WILLIE SAWGRASS

a Novel

AIDA GALE

Palm Beach, Florida

Pineapple Press
Published by Rowman & Littlefield
An imprint of The Rowman & Littlefield Publishing Group, Inc.
4501 Forbes Boulevard, Suite 200, Lanham, Maryland 20706
www.rowman.com

Distributed by NATIONAL BOOK NETWORK

British Library Cataloguing in Publication Information Available

Library of Congress Cataloging-in-Publication Data

Names: Gale, Aida, 1957– author.
Title: Willie Sawgrass / Aida Gale.
Description: Palm Beach, Florida : Pineapple Press, 2021. | Summary: "Willie
 Sawgrass takes place in the wilderness of Southwest Florida in the early
 1900s, when the cattle and fishing industry were strong but rum running
 was more lucrative. Willie isn't sure how old he is when his ignorant
 and abusive Pa sends him away to live with a young Miccosukee woman
 and her son, Nakee, but his adventures are about to start."—Provided by
 publisher.
Identifiers: LCCN 2020050547 (print) | LCCN 2020050548 (ebook) | ISBN
 9781683342656 (trade paperback) | ISBN 9781683342663 (epub)
Subjects: LCSH: Florida—Fiction.
Classification: LCC PS3607.A4117 W55 2021 (print) | LCC PS3607.A4117
 (ebook) | DDC 813/.6—dc23
LC record available at https://lccn.loc.gov/2020050547
LC ebook record available at https://lccn.loc.gov/2020050548

1

Pa never used a surname. Could be he didn't belong to no one, but I reckon he probably just couldn't remember it. Pa was a mean, scanty little man, so simpleminded he could only remember to eat and sleep. He was getting up in years, and I don't think I liked him much but he was all I had. My name is Willie, and I was just a young one when I decided that I wanted a surname. It couldn't be simple like Pa. A surname is what them church ladies say makes a young man respectable, and without one you're a nobody like Pa. I didn't wanna be a nobody like Pa; Black or Smith wouldn't do. I needed a name to be proud of, a name with meaning, a strong name. I thought hard on that for a long time.

It came to me one day as I was looking out across the Glades thinking how safe everything was in that old swamp on account of nobody wanting to mess with them sharp blades on them long green weeds they call sawgrass. Them blades was sharp, not simple like Pa, and they stood tall like me. Them church ladies always said I was growing like a weed. I knew right then that "Sawgrass, Willie Sawgrass," was gonna be my name.

"Ain't nobody's gonna mess with me 'cause I's growing tall and sharper than most," I said to myself as I glanced at an old turtle sunning himself on a log nearby.

I never knew my momma. It was years earlier while I was too little to remember when Momma got so mighty sick she didn't make it through the night. They say it was them skeeters that done her in.

How those tiny, pesky little bugs could make one so sick is they just suck the life right out of you with their thirst for blood. Like little demons working for the devil himself and no amount of praying was gonna make them demons go away.

After Momma passed, Pa and I stayed pretty lean on account of him not knowing how—nor caring—to do much cooking. He said Momma could cook better than any proper church lady, and he told me that I'd better learn to cook as good as Momma or there was no reason to have me around.

We lived on the edge of that big swamp called the Everglades and spent our nights in that one-room shack Pa built from old cypress planks. It had nothing but old wilted palm fronds for a roof and Momma's old tablecloth hanging in the doorway. Pa told me if I didn't keep enough firewood nearby every day, he'd toss me in them hot coals to keep the flames licking the night air. I looked for sticks every day to keep the woodpile stocked. I also made sure that fire burned every night outside our shack, smoking up the place to chase them skeeters away and to keep Pa from tossing me into them hot

coals. We was either smoky or wet sleeping in that shack. Old palm fronds scattered on the roof couldn't keep the water out so when it rained, well, we got wet just like all them other critters in the scrub. We mostly lived on boiled fish and swamp cabbage and an occasional gopher tortoise. We also bartered with the natives on the edge of the reservation from time to time, hoping to get some of that tasty fry bread. Pa hardly ever had anything good for them, but they was just nice enough to give us fry bread for the long walk back to the shack. I had to eat my fry bread real fast to keep Pa from snatching it away from me. The village was a good day's walk into the swampy marshlands so we couldn't go during the rainy season.

Them church ladies in town would send food out our way on Sundays like they promised Momma so as not to let me go to starving. Mostly, I reckon, they did it to keep Pa from getting so mighty hungry I'd be his dinner one night. Pa said Momma was a strong Christian woman and her wallop with a stick and sharp tongue kept him from sinning. He also said that it was to our good fortune that she never missed her day with the Lord on any Sunday to keep us in his good graces.

2

For such a scanty little man Pa had a mean appetite and would eat about anything. Most of his teeth were missing so he'd suck all he could out of them gopher bones till there was hardly nothing left; then he'd lick that wooden plate of his like a dog lappin' up water from a puddle. If there was anything left in the pot, he'd be sticking his hand in it to get the last drop, wiping it real clean.

There was never much for us to eat, but I always made sure Pa got to fill his belly first so as not to let the meanness outta him. I learned early in life while on the receiving end of a belt to limit my rations and never take the last serving from the pot warming over the fire.

I was real young when Pa showed me how to throw a line out for dinner. He insisted most every day that we go to the creek to catch us something to eat. Thinking back on it, I knew Pa was always feeling poorly so he needed a young one along so as to hold the pole while he'd just be napping under that shady cabbage palm.

Pa learned the hard way that he'd better poke a long cane pole up into the tree branches before settling down for his nap. It was on account of what happened one afternoon when we went to the creek to catch us some dinner. Pa stood there stretching his arms before he slid under that tree for his nap. Then, he got down and turned to lay on his back only to have a big mama coon jump out at him. Her babies were up in that tree, and she was gonna have none of Pa moving in on her territory scaring her young ones.

Pa jumped to his feet real fast while I hid behind a scrub palm to watch him wrestle that beast. As I saw it, Pa was on the losing end of that battle. He was screaming and cursing real loud; then he took to scrambling down the bank to the water's edge and back up again. Suddenly, I saw him running down the trail with that coon hanging from his head and Pa's arms flapping all over the place.

I couldn't see where Pa run off to, but I figured he'd eventually be back wanting some dinner. Pa would be mad and hungry after all that excitement, and I was just sure if I didn't catch us something to eat, there was most likely gonna be a whipping so I just stayed there fishing.

I watched them baby coons, clumsy as all get out, climb down that tree and scamper into the scrub. They later came out to chase fiddler crabs on the muddy shore close to where I was fishing. Time passed pretty quick with me watching them baby coons playing around, but them fish just wasn't biting. I hadn't noticed, but it must have been some time since I had any bait on my hook. I began to worry. It was getting late, and Pa always said that with no fire at night we'd be some big cat's dinner and if not, the skeeters would surely eat us alive.

Suddenly, while the sun was drifting lower to the west, I heard Pa yelling and carrying on in the distance. I didn't need to see him to know it was Pa. I could tell he was mad and fit to be tied. That coon must have got the best of him. I listened to him for quite some time before he reached the bend on the trail where I could see him. His yelling grew louder, and there he was walking right at me with his eyes buggin' out and that crazy toothless grin on his face. I was shaking in my pants, getting ready to run, knowing how mad Pa was. That mama coon cut him up good 'cause he was bleeding all over the place. Then I saw it: hanging from his left hand was that coon's tail and hanging from his right one was the rest of it. Pa got himself a prize coon to boil up for dinner that night, and there wasn't gonna be a whipping.

Pa carried on about that coon for weeks, and to hear him tell the story, one would think he'd've been scheming and tracking that coon all day before he got the chance to nab it like any experienced coon hunter. It was all them scabs on his head and missing patches of hair that proved his story was somewhat misleading. Ever since that day Pa always poked that cane pole up into that tree before his nap, just in case.

Coon meat was a good dinner for us, but at that time I was still quite young and getting any food was a difficult chore for me. Pa let me use his hatchet to chop small palms for their tender hearts. He told me that I best not leave the hatchet laying around in the scrub or there was gonna be nothing left when he got done with me. Pa was lazy so he also let me use his old fishing knife to clean fish and cut up the small palm hearts that we ate so much of.

While searching for food in the scrub every day I learned where every huckleberry bush grew. That was a secret I was sure not to tell Pa. I knew he'd cheat me out of them, and it was quite a treat for me when I could sit by myself and eat all them sweet berries off the bushes without having to share. I also had lots of time to practice throwing that old hatchet at a nearby tree. It was heavy for my small hands. I had to stand real close to the tree to throw it, and it wouldn't stick much before it would just drop to the ground with a thump. It was lonely growing up in the scrub, but I made the best of it.

I got pretty good at finding gopher turtles to boil up for soup, and I learned to follow the screeches of a mockingbird with hopes of finding a nest full of eggs in a nearby bush. They're mean birds that attack your head from above when protecting their nest. Getting pecked in the face by birds was painful but, as I saw it, going home empty-handed to take on Pa's hungry belly was more painful.

Mostly I'd bring back the crown of a scrub palm so we could let the fiber dry out for kindling and cut the heart out to feed us. Pa couldn't see too good. His eyes was failing him for some time. One afternoon while I was chopping up that tender palm heart for soup, he pushed me aside and reached down to get himself a piece. Instead, Pa picked up a fat weevil grub and put it in his mouth. Those weevils are a nuisance laying their eggs in palmetto bushes like they do. It didn't kill him, and he said it was the best piece of palm heart he ever ate so I just smiled and gave him more.

3

That old shack we lived in was a ways up the creek to the east side of town. Not much of a town in them days, don't think more than a few people even lived there. It was mostly a place for the fishing boats to dock in the safe little bay. Pa just called it "town." Mostly people had their homestead out in the scrub and just went to town occasionally to see what supplies they could barter for off the fishing boats.

We stayed close to home, but ever so often we'd go down-river in that old wooden skiff Pa found floating in the water after a storm when Momma was still alive. As I grew big enough to hold a paddle, Pa had me pushing it through the water to town and back. Pa always threw a line out in hopes of catching us some fish to cook up for lunch when we got there, in the late morning. Pa would try to find a little work to trade for much-needed supplies back at the shack. Sometimes, we'd take back some smoked mullet or salt. One of the church ladies lived in town. She would let me pick oranges from her tree when they were in season. Sometimes, I'd help her pull weeds from her garden and she'd give me a melon or a couple juicy tomatoes.

That working part didn't happen much for Pa, being as his first stop would be Jack's. That's where the usual men would sit on the back porch drinking and shootin' the breeze about what was going on in our part of the world. Pa always tried to talk someone out of a drink or two. He'd be mighty proud when that worked out, but if not, he'd find himself a shady spot to lay down for a nap then try again later. While Pa was napping, I played around the docks, usually getting in the way of them fishermen. Sometimes there was another kid to play with but not often because they were almost always having to work helping their pas.

Jack got his rum from Cuban sailors who stopped by ever so often on their way to Tampa. Any spirits was bad and illegal in them days, and they'd be in a Tampa jail if they got caught. I saw that Cuban sailing ship tied up to the dock in town a few times. Jack would give them food and a clean bed for the night, and there would always be some nice ladies serving them their food. In return Jack would get some of that Cuban rum to barter with or sell to the locals.

In the clearing beyond Jack's was an old chikee hut with cypress benches that was used for the church ladies' Sunday services. When their husbands was done praying in that place they'd be going to Jack's for a drink or two till their ladies finished Bible study. After the ladies was done studying their Bibles they'd be over at Jack's beating the drunk outta their men and dragging them away to fill their bellies at the afternoon church picnic. Church ladies said they didn't do all that cooking to have their men drinking all afternoon. Pa said those ladies were always praying for us so there was no need for us to be in town much on Sundays.

I didn't mind going to town, 'cause while I was paddling back to the shack Pa was full of stories to tell of a time before me and before he married Momma. Stories about fishing, sailing ships, and pirates. There was a time in Pa's life when he was working on a fishing boat in the Florida Bay and fighting with Greek sponge divers. He always said Greeks were pirates! Back at the shack he'd sometimes ramble on for days about how the pirates jilted him of his fortune when he was on a drunk one night in Key West. He said he had a full twelve dollars in his pocket. More money than he ever had at one time and the pirates took it from him. I asked if he might have drunk his way to an empty pocket, but another lesson I learned was to never bring up that consideration again.

Sometimes if Pa didn't approve of my actions he'd say he was gonna sell me off as slimy bait to the fishermen in town or he'd have someone drag me away and sell me to the pirates. I don't mind saying at that young age the thought of it scared the pants off me. Pa said he'd buy a worthless old maid with the money 'cause an old maid couldn't be worth no more than a boy and any old maid could clean fish and cook better than a boy could. He brought that up in town once, and I was mighty relieved when the fishermen laughed at Pa, telling him I wasn't worth not even a penny. I suppose it was on account of Pa always telling folks I was just a good-for-nothing kid and he'd be better off not having me around to take care of. The way I saw it, being a worthless kid was a good thing; it's what kept me safe at home. Our trips to town and back is how I came to know about fishing, sailing ships, and pirates.

4

It was early on a Sunday afternoon when Pa and me heard the chattering church ladies coming up the trail. Something in their loud voices told us they were up to no good. Sure enough, they came all dressed in their Sunday's best wearing big flowery hats and carrying big white purses and picnic baskets. They didn't just come to bring us food. They came to chatter about school.

Well, I don't need to say how that got Pa all worked up to yelling at the ladies. He told them if they didn't skedaddle out of there, he was gonna sic the gators on them. The church ladies were insistent that they knew what was best for me and that I was gonna go to school to get me an education.

"There's a new teacher in town, 'n we signed Willie up to get educated!" one yelled.

"We're here to tell ya that ya best get him to the chikee church bright 'n early Monday mornin' to get him some schoolin'!" another demanded sharply.

By then I was squirming, trying to get away from the tight hold of one of those ladies while another, with her glove off, was licking her fingers and wiping the dirt off my face.

"This boy needs a bath!" she shouted at Pa.

"Poor Willie," another said sadly as she looked down at me and patted my head.

Right then Pa got so mad he grabbed a palm frond off the ground and started hollering and shooing those ladies down the path with it. Them ladies was screaming mad, and one turned to Pa with her eyes open real wide and her mouth scrunched up so tight she looked like she just bit into a lemon. She pointed her finger at the sky and looked at me, then back at Pa.

"You best be going to church on Sundays or you'll be seeing the devil one day!" she threatened loudly; then she turned and scurried away with the rest of the ladies.

I didn't understand that devil part much, but it scared me anyway. I knew Pa wasn't about to do anything if it was an inconvenience, and getting me to school would surely be an inconvenience.

Attempts to get me an education had been tried before, but that didn't worry me none. Them ladies kept sending away for teachers from a church in a place called Jacksonville, and no sooner than one would arrive she'd get a notion to get outta this place quick. I heard teachers were proper and civilized and couldn't take the hard life in the scrub with skeeters, snakes, and gators. The church ladies didn't stand a chance of getting me an education with the teachers always running off. According to the church ladies, we was going to be uncivilized till they got one to stay.

Pa never went to school, and he said that going to school wasn't something I'd be much interested in. We weren't even sure what uncivilized was, but if it meant me not going to school, then uncivilized was just fine by us.

5

Living with Pa, a man meaner than a mama coon with babies up a tree, wasn't easy but I learned mighty young to keep my distance when I could. I grew to be a bit smarter than Pa and always one step ahead of him so as not to cause myself any trouble.

As I got older Pa decided I wasn't worth keeping around anymore. With me not doing all he wanted me to do and sometimes not able to keep from speaking my mind at him, he decided one day

that he was gonna pass me on to a Miccosukee girl in the Indian village who Pa called "Tayki." I didn't want to go because life at the shack was all I knew, but he insisted, and with belt in hand he took me anyway.

I knew it wouldn't take long for the church ladies to catch wind that Pa didn't have a young one around anymore and they'd put a stop to sending food out his way on Sundays. I'll bet he was mighty sorry he sent me away when that happened. It wasn't until the following year, when by chance, I got word that travelers came upon Pa's remains along the trail north of the shack with nothing but buzzards keeping him company. They said that with so little food and moving on in years, Pa withered away to nothing. While too weak to care for himself he fell prey to a roaming panther.

Tayki didn't seem old enough to have a young one of her own when I came to be with her in that Miccosukee village. She was cast aside in the village due to the fact that her baby came out with dark skin and straight black hair but eyes bluer than the sky on a sunny day. The native elders called him "Ah-naht-kee whaunan cheh," which meant nonhuman boy. They knew that like me he was nonhuman because his seed came from a white man. I just called that blue-eyed nonhuman boy "Nakee."

The village was in a reservation upriver from the big sea they call the Gulf of Mexico. Tayki lived in the swamp at the edge of the village, and life was hard for her with us boys and no man around to help. At first, I felt a bit lost living there, not understanding what anyone was saying and knowing that they didn't want me, but after a while, I began to feel a responsibility for Tayki and Nakee and that place became home for me. I helped Tayki as much as I could and was mighty grateful to her for cooking our fish and making us fry bread with beans and squash from her garden.

I learned some of their words, and Nakee was young and learned some of my words. Somehow we were able to communicate and he could tell me what the natives were saying. I liked having him around to talk to and do things with. He grew to depend on me, and I willingly took care of and watched over him. We were always

16

Kevin
Hutchinson

together and grew up with a tighter bond than any true brothers could ever have, us being nonhuman and all.

I never knew my age when Pa took me to live at the village, but if I was to guess I'd say I was about eight or nine due to the fact it was gonna be a few years before I'd see the changes that happen when a boy grows into his early manhood years. As for Nakee, he had just lost his first tooth.

The boys of the village weren't too friendly to Nakee and me, and I found myself not liking them much either. Nakee said those boys insisted we nonhumans didn't belong in the village, and they said they were going to make sure to run us out of there. Nakee was too small, so I felt alone defending us from their evil ways.

The native boys were good hunters. They learned from the men of the village. Pa never taught me anything but to hold a cane pole over the water, paddle a skiff, and start a fire. I learned almost everything else on my own. I didn't like it much when the native boys laughed and made fun of me. Sometimes they'd come by our chikee carrying a deer or a hog hanging upside down by its feet from a pole. They'd walk by us laughing because they knew we weren't going to get any. I knew that deer was gonna be real tasty and good for those boys, and I was just wishing I could catch us a deer to eat.

By the time Pa brought me to the village I'd got pretty good making the hatchet stick to that tree in the scrub by the huckleberry bushes. I knew where Pa kept it, so I decided right then that since Pa wasn't going to need it, I was going back to the shack to get me a hatchet.

6

While living back at the shack I got real good at sneaking around to keep Pa from yelling at me, so the next day I got up real early without waking up Nakee or Tayki. I sneaked away from the village so quiet even the dogs didn't hear me leave. It was still dark with just a sliver of a moon in the sky to light up the trail, but the sun would be rising soon enough. It had been a long time since Pa made me leave the shack. I was confident when I set out that morning that I could find my way, but it was getting late and I wasn't real sure anymore which way to go. I figured sometime during the day I had gone off the trail because I should have been at the shack already. I felt hungry and somewhat concerned. I had to start looking for a place to camp so I could get a fire started. I kept walking when suddenly I wandered into a big low-lying grassy area and there were cows there!

I stood there watching the cows graze on the green grass when suddenly I got poked in my side and about jumped out of my pants. I turned around quick to see a mean-looking man with a rifle in his hands standing next to me. He asked me what I was doing.

"Nothin', sir, I's just watchin' them cows," I said.

He was one of them real tough cracker cowmen herding cows north to sell. That man grabbed me by the collar, jerked me around, and pushed me forward so hard I fell to my knees. As I jumped to my feet real quick, he pushed me again and insisted on walking me back to his camp where more cowmen were sitting around a fire. I could smell something mighty good cooking in a pot.

"I found me a scrawny little boy lookin' to take one of our cows," the man with the rifle said.

"No sir! I wasn't!" I hollered at him. I added, "I'm hungry, mista. I'd be much obliged if you could spare me some leftovers. Sure smells good, 'n I haven't ate all day." I knew I was begging, but I was so hungry I didn't care.

"Feed the kid and send him on his way," one man said, sounding somewhat annoyed.

"You best leave them cows alone, kid," another one shouted over at me.

"Yes sir, mistuh, 'n thank ya," I replied.

I never ate food that good in my life. It was real beef stew, and lots of it, with potatoes and carrots. They even gave me bread to wipe the plate clean, and it sure didn't need washing when I was done. That food was so good I didn't ever want to leave, but they told me I'd best be on my way in the morning. They didn't want me tagging along, so the next morning they pointed me in the right direction and I started walking. Those cowmen weren't too friendly, but it was my good fortune I ran into them for a good meal and a safe place to sleep.

I walked all morning, thinking about how good that beef stew was the night before. I also thought about Nakee and how much he might not like me going away without telling him. Tayki depended on me too and was probably wondering where I'd gone off to. Maybe they were worried about me. I thought about how good that made me feel. I never felt like that before.

As I walked things began to look familiar. The trail was over-grown, but I knew it was the way to the shack and I started walking faster, almost running. I got to the bend near Pa's spot where we spent so many afternoons fishing, and I knew I was getting close. I recognized the tree where that coon caused such a ruckus that one day. On the other side of the creek I saw Pa's old, waterlogged skiff next to a mangrove half-sunk with an old tree laying on top of it.

I was so excited to be back home, I started thinking of Pa in a way I never had before. I wondered what his life was like as a young one growing up in the scrub and who his momma and pa were. He was gone, and for the first time ever in my life, I felt sad for him, true as can be.

Before I knew it, I was standing in front of the shack. It wasn't there. It was there, but it wasn't. It was in pieces scattered all over the place. Over time those afternoon winds must have blown it apart. I could see what was left of the old tablecloth that always hung in the doorway. It was torn and tangled in a palmetto bush, and standing next to it were two cabbage palms with a couple of cypress planks wedged between them. As I looked around I could see where the fire had burned every night keeping the skeeters away. Laying there, half-filled with sand and a metal spoon stuck in the sand, was the pot we boiled that coon in. We boiled up lots of swamp cabbage and fish in that pot too. I dumped the sand out and put the spoon inside so I could take it back for Tayki. I spent a long time looking for the hatchet but didn't have any luck finding it. I also looked for the knife but no luck there either.

It was getting late and the sun was going down, so I gathered some of the cypress planks and made a lean-to next to the firepit. I took that old, half-rotted tablecloth and put it on the ground for me to lay on. I needed kindling to start the fire, so I reached down next to a palmetto bush to get some fiber when I grabbed hold of something hard and heavy. I moved it out of the way when I realized it was the hatchet head. It was rusted, and without the handle, it blended in with all that palm fiber, and that's why I couldn't find it. I got the fire started and settled down to sleep. I wanted to get an early start in the morning, but I was excited and could only think of getting back to the village to start working on my hatchet. I was real tired, though, and soon drifted off to sleep.

I woke up the next morning to the sound of pesky skeeters buzzing in my ears. It was early and I was ready to head back. With the fire almost out, not making much smoke, the skeeters were biting something fierce. I could only look around at that shack that wasn't there with much sadness, but I remembered some good times too. I couldn't understand the reason for such confusion in my head, but I didn't have any more time to think about it. I turned away, took the cooking pot by the handle, and put the old tablecloth in the pot with the spoon and rusty hatchet head. I couldn't help glancing back one last time before heading down the trail.

It would take all day to get back to the village, and I had not eaten since I met up with the crackers two nights before. My belly was feeling empty and starting to hurt. I remembered that delicious beef stew and could only wish for more to eat before nightfall.

I'd been walking all morning without incident when I began hearing lots of splashing in the distance. I couldn't see anything through the brush, so I set the pot down by the trunk of a small waxy myrtle tree and climbed up, expecting to see two gators going at it in a fight. I could see the shallow creek from the tree, and there were mullet jumping and splashing all over the place. Some of them were landing and flopping all around on the muddy banks on both sides with gators scooping them up. There were too many gators around for me to try to get my share of fish, but just then one fell from the sky onto the ground next to the tree I was in. I looked up only to see the osprey that dropped the fish soaring down to pick it up. Without thinking, I jumped from that tree right onto the fish before the bird could swoop it up, but with its talons out, it snagged me instead just as I landed. I felt the stinging pain as it sliced the back of my shoulder good; then suddenly I was bleeding all over me and my fish. I think that osprey was as surprised to see me jump out of that tree as I was to see a fish fall from the sky.

The old tablecloth came in handy to wrap my bleeding shoulder but didn't stop it from hurting. It was hard for me to gather kindling and start a fire with my shoulder still bleeding and hurting so bad. I could feel the pain all the way down to my hand, but after a while, I managed to get the fire going. I struggled to skewer the fish with a green palm frond stick; then I cooked it and ate it. I must say, right then, that fish tasted good as beef stew.

7

I had walked all day and it was getting dark, but I could see the glow on the horizon from the fires in the village and I knew I'd be there soon. The dogs barked at me, causing a disturbance when I got there; then I saw Nakee run out of the chikee toward me.

"Willie!" he yelled excitedly.

I could tell he was happy to see me as he grabbed my arm and squeezed it. Then, to my surprise, he began punching me and crying.

"Why you leave me? You scare me!" he screamed at me as tears streamed down his face.

Tayki came running behind him. She grabbed Nakee, and after giving me a stern look, she pulled him away. I could tell she was really mad, and I never felt so bad over anything before in my life. I stood there limp and confused at what I did wrong; I figured, maybe it was because I was gone too long. I wondered what to do next when just then the pot slid out of my hand. It hit the ground with a clank that got my attention.

I quickly looked up at Tayki dragging Nakee away by his arm. I reached down, grabbed the pot with the spoon in it, then I took the hatchet head out with my other hand and ran after them, calling for them to stop. As I got close Tayki turned around real fast and, holding Nakee by her side crying, gave me a real tongue lashing. I couldn't understand what she was saying, but I knew she was scolding me bad. I quickly held out the pot for her, and she stopped. She looked at the pot, then at me, then at the pot again. She grabbed it from my hand, and with a smile she pulled Nakee with her and ran to the chikee to admire her new pot in front of the fire. I followed them to the chikee and saw Nakee, sitting on a mat, pretending to be eating with the metal spoon. He looked at me teary eyed and smiled. I had made amends.

Later that evening when Tayki was done cleaning and admiring the old metal pot and spoon, she noticed my hurt shoulder. By then the pain had reached its peak for me and I was laying, chest down, on the sleeping mat. Tayki came over to tend to my cut shoulder while I told Nakee what happened. Tayki was use to fixing our skinned knees, cuts, and bruises, but this was a deep wound. She tried her best but didn't really know what to do. The pain was so bad I could hardly sleep that night, but by morning even the skeeters couldn't wake me, so I slept until early afternoon. I woke up hungry, but my shoulder wasn't hurting so bad. There was a clean wrap around my shoulder thanks to Tayki. At daybreak she had gone to see the village medicine man and brought back a potion for my wound then wrapped it real good while I slept.

Tayki gave me fry bread and boiled fish with beans from the garden, and while I was eating, the native boys walked by, yelling and laughing at me because they'd heard I'd been hurt. I couldn't understand what they were saying. Nakee told me that they had heard what happened and said that it was too bad that osprey didn't drop me from the sky into a gator pond. They also said I should go away and never come back. I didn't like those boys being so mean to me, but that's how it was.

8

I started cleaning the rust off my hatchet with a rock, and even with that potion on my shoulder, it was still too painful to do much that evening. I did the best I could, but it took most of the next three days to scrape through some of the rust to where the clean metal was finally starting to shine through. None of the village boys had a metal hatchet. They just had shell hatchets.

It took many days for most of the pain in my shoulder to go away, and there was a nasty scab on it. I knew it was gonna leave a mean-looking scar in that spot, but I didn't mind because I could show it off as a sign of bravery. No native boy had a scar as good as mine, and I was proud of that.

The hatchet head was finally clean and shiny. It was ready for me to sharpen it up. I was glad that metal was thick and strong so there was something left by the time I got done scraping all the rust off. I was ready to put a handle on it, but there wasn't much good wood nearby to make it from. I needed hardwood, so I decided to take Nakee with me to look for some. I remembered resting in the shade of a big live oak on my trip back from the shack. There would surely be a good strong branch there to make a handle with. It would take a couple of hours walking to get there, and Nakee had never been so far from the village. He was excited to go, but I told him we had to keep it a secret from Tayki.

I tested the sharp blade of my hatchet again before we left because even without a handle it would be useful for chipping away at that oak tree to get me a good branch. Nakee and me headed north up the trail. It was a real hot day and Nakee kept lagging behind, so it took a bit longer than I had planned. I just hoped Tayki wouldn't notice us being gone so long. There were tall pine trees in the distance, and I knew that old oak tree was just past them. As we got close we smelled a faint scent of something not so good.

"I smell skunk," Nakee said.

Sure enough, I knew that smell, and that's what it was.

We sneaked up real close only to find, not just one, but a whole family of skunks rummaging around some scrub palms next to that big oak. It was probably full of weevil grubs and palmetto bugs, and the skunks were filling their bellies.

"How's we gonna get rid of them critters?" I asked Nakee as he crouched down behind me.

Just then he stood up real quick with a pinecone in his hand and threw it at them real hard. We were both quite surprised when two big old skunks came running at us with their tails sticking way up in the air. They were spraying a haze of smell all over the place, and we were right in the middle of it.

"Nakee! What'd you do that for!" I screamed at him as I took off running down the trail fast as I could.

Nakee was running and screaming behind me, trying to keep up.

We ran for a long time before stopping. I turned to scold Nakee good for what he did, but when I looked at him, he looked real funny with his nose all crinkled up in his face and his eyes blinking real fast. All I could do was laugh at him. He didn't like that much because the spray was burning his eyes.

"Serves ya right, and don't ya ever be doin' nothin' like that again! How's we gonna get this smell off us?" I scolded him as he waved one hand in front of his crinkled-up nose and used the other to wipe his watering eyes.

I waited until Nakee's eyes were feeling better; then we both cautiously wandered back to the oak tree. The skunks were gone, and we could barely stand the smell around there, but I wasn't going back to the village empty-handed. I searched the tree for a good branch to take and spotted one on the second limb up. I climbed the tree and began chipping away at the base of the branch. It took some time, but finally, with a crack it fell to the ground and we were ready to head back.

We dragged that branch down the trail to the village and into the chikee. I was too tired to start whittling and we were both hungry, so I just put it aside and rested. Tayki wasn't around, so we waited for her to get back to have dinner, but when she got back we were in some big trouble. She came in holding her nose, and when she saw my hatchet handle branch, she picked it up and started swinging it and yelling at us to get outta there. I supposed she was gonna have none of us stinking up the place. We ran away from there fast, and she threw my hatchet handle branch right out behind us. Then, she dragged our sleeping mats out away from the chikee for us to sleep on.

Tayki's yelling caught the attention of one of the village boys from across the way, and he couldn't wait to run and tell the others. They all gathered at a distance and started laughing and making fun of us. Nakee said they were calling us skunk boys and I sure didn't like that none 'cause now we were gonna be nonhuman skunk boys. I chased them around the village, hoping to wipe the smell on them and Nakee followed, but they had a good start and were faster than us so we couldn't catch them. At a distance we saw them hopping around on all fours with their bottom ends up in the air pretending to be skunks and they were throwing sand in the air to make it look like spray. They started yelling their native battle cries at us, and there was nothing I could do to stop them. Finally, they got tired of us and went on their way, leaving Nakee and me standing there alone and stinky. I was humiliated and real tired of them getting the best of us. We needed to go to the creek to rinse the stink off us, but before we got too far Tayki came over and threw some weeds at us. They were tied up in two small bunches. She yelled something at us and held out two long, colorful shirts. Nakee picked up the weeds and said we were to wash with them. I grabbed the shirts from Tayki, and the two of us walked to the creek to wash ourselves with weeds.

On our way back to the chikee, we dropped our stinky clothes by a bush with hopes that Tayki might be nice enough to wash them. She set food out on a log for us, but it didn't taste too good. All we could taste was skunk stink.

Tayki made us wash with weeds every morning, and after a few days, either the smell wasn't so bad anymore or we were just use to it, I wasn't sure. She let us bring our sleeping mats back in the chikee, and Nakee and me went back to spending mornings working in the garden and gathering food. I spent the afternoons working on my hatchet handle, and before long, I had whittled that branch down good. It wasn't easy, but I finally got it done and it fit real good, so I pounded a wedge in it tight so it wouldn't come off. I was mighty proud of my metal hatchet.

A metal hatchet was hard to come by, and I understood why Pa told me there'd be nothing left of me if I was to lose it. I took it with me everywhere and kept it under my sleeping mat ever night. I practiced throwing my hatchet ever day after lunch, and I don't mind saying I was getting real good at making it stick to trees. Sometimes it would stick so hard even Nakee and me together could barely pull it out. My aim was getting good too. I'd be making it stick in the same spot most every throw.

9

We always kept our distance from any gators we saw, but one day I got it in my head to show the native boys up. I was gonna get us a gator for dinner and show them how brave I was. Nakee and me finished our work in the garden then took a long walk down the trail to a wide, sharp bend in the river. We saw some gators sunning themselves on the banks of the shallow water. I looked for a tree like the one I climbed by the mullet creek on my way back from the shack. There was one tree that leaned over the water and was far enough away from the gators that they wouldn't see us. It was a good spot, so we climbed it quietly and watched. We spent a few hours every day, for three days, watching the gators from that tree. There were so many of them, and they all had their own sunning spots. We picked a gator that was a little bigger than me, just right for dinner with plenty left for jerky. It laid on the bank of the river just far enough away from some mangroves that I could hide behind. I thought it would be an easy target. It occurred to me that if I didn't get him good he might run into the water with my hatchet and I'd never see it again. I had to think more on that because that was a problem I would have to solve first.

After dinner I was sitting next to the fire admiring my hatchet. I was mighty proud of it, and the thought of losing it made my stomach real uneasy. I couldn't get it out of my head how I was gonna get that gator without losing my hatchet. I stared and stared at it when I came across the idea to tie a rope around it so I could fish it out if it was to wind up in the water. I needed a long piece of rope, and the natives in the village were real good at making strong rope.

The next morning I took Nakee with me and we went rope hunting around the village. Most everyone was shooing us away like we were flies, but we finally ran into some luck. One of the native women was nice to us and gave me a real long piece of rope. She had it coiled up on a peg in her chikee. The other bit of luck was, the native boys didn't bother us none because they were out hunting. I was mighty grateful to that woman and I thanked her a lot.

I took the rope back to the chikee and started thinking about how a long time ago when I was playing on the docks in town, one of the fishermen was real good at showing me how to tie a knot he called a bowline, and I needed that knowledge now. I tried tying the rope for a while but could only get it tangled with unwanted knots. When I got a little better at it I ran that rope across that hatchet head back and forth and around the handle a few times, but I couldn't get it right so I coiled it up and went to get help from that woman who gave it to me. She wrapped one end of the rope around the handle a bunch of times real neat and tight in a way that it couldn't come off. I thanked the rope lady a lot for helping me; then I went back to the chikee and hurried to finish my work in the garden. I couldn't wait to practice throwing my hatchet with the rope on it. It was different and the rope kept tangling up, but after a few days, with Nakee watching, I was starting to get the hang of it. I was gonna have to hit that gator real hard on the head and kill it fast so it wouldn't run off.

After a couple of weeks I was feeling brave and skilled enough to go after the gator we picked. Nakee and me walked down to that spot in the river, and I told him to get up in the tree real quietly while I sneaked over behind the mangroves close to our gator. He was just laying there sunning himself with his mouth open. He sure had some sharp teeth. I could only think of him running away with my hatchet if I didn't kill him fast, so I put it down and quietly tied the loose end of the rope around my waist. I picked my hatchet up real slow and waited patiently; then I lifted it over my head and took careful aim. He gently closed his mouth, and his eyes started to open real slow. I think he sensed that something was up, and he started to move a little. I quickly ran toward him and threw my hatchet at him. I missed my mark and could see that I struck him between his neck and his front leg. The hatchet stuck real good because when that gator whipped around to jump in the water, the rope wrapped around him and he jerked me hard; then he started pulling me behind him. The other gators were startled and jumped into the water. I didn't want to be pulled in to be eaten by a bunch of mean gators, so I dug my feet into the sand and pulled for my life.

"Pull, Willie, pull!" Nakee yelled as he scrambled down the tree.

"I'm pullin'! Help me!" I yelled back. "Help! He's gonna pull me in!" I screamed, hoping Nakee could somehow save me.

Nakee ran to me, grabbed my pants, and started pulling. He was trying to help when all of a sudden that gator turned. The rope loosened, and he started coming after us.

"Run, Nakee! He's gonna get us! Run!" I screamed.

Nakee let go and started running away, and I was running behind him when the gator suddenly stopped. The rope tightened and quickly yanked me backward, and I fell to the ground. Nakee looked back and started screaming while I got up real quick. I was trying to untie the rope from around my waist, but that beast turned and started dragging me. That gator was going back to the water, and I was pulling for my life all over again. With me pulling against him and Nakee screaming, the gator reared his head up as it jerked itself around and started after us again. He couldn't run real good with that hatchet in him, and the rope was tangled around his leg and his neck. There was a small waxy myrtle in front of me, so as I ran past it I went around once and jumped onto a branch only a few feet above the ground, but my foot got caught tight between the rope and the tree. I was up there watching the gator just below me rolling in the sand wrapping itself up in the rope. I wasn't sure what to do next. I could see my hatchet stuck deep in him. I must have hit him hard enough to make it stick into a bone. He was bleeding a lot, and I thought maybe he'd bleed out and die, so I just waited. I was in the tree trying to get the knot undone from around my waist. I needed to loosen it to free my foot from the rope around my ankle.

All of a sudden Nakee yelled real loud, "He's chewing the rope!"

I looked down, and that gator had the rope in his mouth.

"Nakee!" I shouted. "Throw sand in his face! Throw it in his mouth, but if it gets loose, you run!"

I was getting real scared that if it chewed the rope through, that gator would walk my hatchet right into the water.

"Get a long stick and shove it in his mouth! Do something!" I screamed.

I kept scrambling to get loose, but the rope was too tight. Nakee was real brave and ran to that gator with his two hands full of sand. He threw it in its face and quick ran away; then he crouched down, shoved his hands into the sand, and started flinging it up at the gator's face, but he was too far away. By then the gator was rolling in the sand again and managed to unwrap the rope from around its neck, and that was giving the rope some slack, maybe enough for me to get my foot loose.

I saw my gator back up a little, but he was getting tired and weak from bleeding out. The sand around him was soaked with blood. His belly was laying flat on the ground, and he wasn't moving much. I hung down from the branch to give the rope more slack. It was hurting my ankle real bad. I needed to get the knot undone to get my foot loose and get out of the tree. I watched the gator carefully because I knew he could reach me if I hung down too low. Finally, when I got free, I tied the rope to the tree and began lowering myself real careful. I jumped to the ground and fell because of the pain in my ankle, but I got up quick and ran as fast as I could from the tree. I turned only to see that gator's tail sway to the side and its back claw dig into the sand, but it was getting weak. Nakee was still flinging sand all over the place, so I yelled at him to stop.

I rested a bit as I rubbed some of the pain out of my foot; then I jumped back up into the tree to untie the rope from the branch. I worked it around the tree, unwrapping it, and below I could see how the rope was real slack, but the gator didn't pull or move much anymore. Nakee grabbed a long stick and started poking at one of his eyes. I was scared for Nakee and yelled for him to leave him alone. The gator slowly moved his head sideways to get away from Nakee's stick, but by then it was clear that it was dying from losing so much blood. I got down from the tree and my ankle was feeling better, so we started to pull on the rope. It didn't pull against us, so together Nakee and me tried to drag our catch back to the chikee. The gator rolled one more time, and the rope unwrapped from around its neck. We pulled and pulled, but it was too heavy and we were hot and tired. We kept pulling when suddenly, the hatchet let loose. I fell forward and Nakee sprung forward too, hitting me in the back with his head. The hatchet finally came out, slingshotted forward, and landed in front of the gator.

We sat down to rest and watched it for a while. I coiled the rope, pulling my hatchet toward me; then I untied the rope from the hatchet and handed it to Nakee. The gator had suffered enough. I wanted to make sure it was dead before we got near it. It didn't move much anymore, so I thought if I could hit it one more time from a close distance I could kill it for sure. It was dying and too weak to run off. I walked toward it, holding my hatchet up high and ready to throw, when Nakee ran right past me with a hand full of sand and threw it in his face. I yelled at him to get back, and I took aim at a spot on the back of the gator's neck where his spine was; then I threw real hard and hit my target. He flung his head up and opened his mouth real wide as he took one last gasp of air; then his jaw hit the ground and slapped closed. Our chosen gator was dead.

Nakee and me each picked up a front leg and slowly dragged it between us. It took a while, but we finally got it to the village, and some dogs came over to sniff around at our catch. The native boys saw what we had done but ignored us while they went about their business making paddles. A couple of native men had just come back from the open water, and they were taking two big fish out of their dugout and didn't even look at us. I was disappointed when after we did all that brave gator hunting those boys didn't even care.

At least I knew Tayki would be happy to see what we got for dinner. She was tending to the garden as we struggled to carry the gator to her. When she saw what we had done, she ran straight to me and started slapping me on the head. I didn't understand, but Nakee said she was mad because we were too young to be killing gators and we could have been eaten. She told Nakee to tell me that I best not ever do anything like that again. I promised her I wouldn't.

The three of us worked on cleaning the gator, and Tayki salted the meat up real good and wrapped it in a blanket. It was too late in the day to hang it out to dry, so that would have to wait till morning. Nakee and me each got a front gator foot to put out to dry in the morning, and we cut the claws out of the two back feet and hung them like beads on strings around our necks. We were real proud of that. I kept two claws and put them aside to take to the woman we got the rope from. I wanted to thank her again for being so kind. We cleaned the gator's head and tied the rope through its jaw so we could put it in a shallow spot in the creek for the little fish and crabs to finish cleaning. A few days later it was a real clean gator skull, so we put it in the sun to dry then hung it in our chikee. It looked real good hanging up on a pole.

Tayki was real happy to have gator meat for dinner that night. It was good with squash and beans from the garden. I think she was real proud of Nakee and me but wasn't gonna tell us that. I was still thinking of the native boys just working on their stupid paddles not paying us no mind when suddenly I got a notion to make us our own dugout. It's better than making paddles and safer than killing gators.

10

Since I came to live in the village I'd noticed that someone had once started burning out the center of a cypress log to make a dugout. It was sitting at the edge of the other side of the village, and the mangroves had grown up around it. I needed to know who owned it and ask if we could have it.

It turns out that the native man who started burning out the log got a strange sickness and died a few years back. The village people said the log had evil spirits, and that's why nobody wanted it. I sent Nakee to tell them that we wanted it and since we were nonhumans we wouldn't get sick.

It took a couple of days before they agreed to give it to us. I don't think they really cared if we got sick or not. They probably thought it would give them good reason to be rid of us. It was going to take some time to get that thing to our chikee because we had to chop the mangroves away from it first to move it. Then we had to roll it around the edge of the village to our chikee where we could work on it.

The evil spirits were good to us because they got us that dugout log and kept them village boys away, but I was hoping we wouldn't get that strange sickness too. My hatchet came in real handy for chopping the mangrove limbs while Nakee dragged them away. After it was all cleared we used a pole to pry the burned-out log over the stumps. We worked all day on that and even convinced Tayki to help us pull the rope to get it out from the stumps. Once it was

cleared we pried and pushed real hard to get it to roll, but that too
wasn't easy. It would roll a bit then turn and stop; then we had to
use the pry pole to turn it, and again it would roll, turn, and stop.
This went on all afternoon until we gave up for the day and decided
to get back at it in the morning.

The next morning I could see the native boys standing in the
distance, laughing and pointing at us, but I didn't care. I was gonna
get that log to our chikee. Finally later that day, after pushing, pry-
ing, and rolling it, we had it laying alongside our chikee close to the
water. We were ready to start working on that old cypress log to
make us a real dugout canoe of our own.

Chipping out the old, burnt, and weathered coals inside the log
was pretty easy, but when it was all out we had to start chipping away
at the wood. I used my hatchet while Nakee used a sharp shell, but it
was too hard and taking too long. We needed to start a small fire in
it and burn more of the center out. We put wet sand on some palm
fronds next to us to put on the parts we didn't want burned.

We let the wood burn for a while; then we'd put the fire out
and start chipping at the coals. When the coals were out we had to

let it dry before we could start burning to chip more coals out; then we'd do it all again and again. Every morning we had to help Tayki with the garden, so it took a long time burning and chipping before we had the inside hollowed out enough to start shaping the outside of the log.

Finally we needed to let our hands rest and blisters heal before we started working again. We were real tired of that old log and went off to do other things. After a few weeks, although I wasn't too eager to get back at it, I was determined to get it done. We began working on the dugout again, but Nakee was tired of it and decided he'd rather sweep the chikee or help Tayki in the garden, so I finished all the burning and chipping by myself. I was mighty thankful to him anyway for the helpful work he did.

When it was finished, Nakee and me stood admiring our dugout. When I looked over at him, he smiled at me with those big blue eyes, and below that smile were the gator claws hanging on the string around his neck. I was holding my hatchet, feeling mighty proud of all the things we had done. I wondered if Pa would have been proud of me too.

11

That woman who gave us the rope told us that we still had work to do. She said that we needed to get sap from a Chaka tree and coat our canoe with it to keep it safe from wood boring shipworms. She said that the sap also kept evil spirits away. So right then I knew we needed some of that Chaka sap in case there might be evil spirits in that wood. There were lots of Chaka trees in the hammocks in the Glades, and some were scattered around the village. We were lucky to even have two of them close to our chikee, so Nakee and me worked on getting some sap.

After chopping two wedges out of the bottom of the trunks we put big leaves on the ground next to them to collect the sap that would seep out. The next day we were disappointed when we saw that those trees didn't give us more than a couple of handfuls of sap. We got what was there and started smearing it on the wood anyway, and it didn't take long before we were a real sticky mess. Tayki didn't like what we had done and was yelling at us for all the sticky mess we made in the chikee. We tried as best we could to get that sticky mess cleaned up, but it seemed to spread more. We even tried using sand to scrub it off, but the sand just stuck to us and made it worse. The first few mornings after that, Nakee and me would wake up stuck to our sleeping mats. Tayki had to yank the mats off us, and that hurt a lot. She even had to cut off some of our hair to get us unstuck. We were tired of everything being sticky all the time until it finally wore off.

Our dugout looked a little rough, but it was the best we could do and at least it wasn't so heavy as when it was mostly just a log. It took a lot of pushing and pulling for us to get it to the edge of the creek. Then we managed to get it into the water, and it floated real nice. I cut a piece of rope to tie around my waist where I could secure my hatchet so it wouldn't accidentally fall overboard. We might need it in case a gator came too close. Gators stayed away from the village, and if they did come around they'd get killed real quick by an experienced hunter. We both got in our dugout carefully, keeping the weight of our bodies down low; then with a long pole we pushed ourselves around the shallow places in the creek. I put a hole in the front toward the top of the dugout so we could tie the rope to it; then we tied the other end to the mangroves and just floated out there fishing. I was glad it was so stable 'cause Nakee was always moving around in that thing.

The pole we used to push us around the creek worked real well, but we needed paddles if we were to go farther down to open water. I cut short cypress poles and with my hatchet chipped away the end

of one pole until the wood was flat. I was good with a paddle being as Pa would have me paddling that old skiff of his when he needed me to. I tied the rope from the dugout to a mangrove trunk in the shallow creek nearby and let Nakee practice paddling around while I sat in the dugout making the other paddle. Finally, we had a dugout and two paddles, but it was the time of the year when the afternoon storms would start blowing in and we had to pay attention to the weather.

After eating a good meal one early morning and helping in the garden real fast, I stuck my hatchet into the rope around my waist and Nakee and me set out to go fishing for the first time downriver. Once we reached the open water the current helped us move along farther than we had intended to go. We didn't pay much attention to that because we were having a great time fishing and enjoying the day drifting around in our dugout. It was early in the afternoon when we saw dark clouds in the distance and knew we needed to head back. We paddled for a while, snaking our way around small islands, but we couldn't find the entrance to the river that would take us back to our creek. Neither one of us knew how to navigate around the islands, and they all looked the same. Before long we were lost and getting real tired of paddling.

The water was getting choppy, and a cool breeze was blowing in our faces. We could smell the rain coming. Dark clouds were rolling toward us with loud cracks of lightning and thunder. The tide was up so there was no sandy beach to go to, and the mangroves were so thick on every one of the islands, it didn't matter where we went. I finally just grabbed a strong branch and tied up; then we climb through the mangroves to find some good branches to hunker down on and wait for the storm to pass.

The wind started blowing the branches all around us, so we held on real tight to keep from slipping off. Suddenly the rain started coming down real hard. We didn't wear shirts most of the time, and that day was no exception. The rainwater was cold and stinging our skin real bad. It was like a bunch of dried-up pine needles poking at us. We were huddled together real close trying to keep warm, and

I could hardly open my eyes with all that wind and rain blowing in my face. If I tried real hard I could look through the branches and see the waves bouncing our dugout up and down against the mangroves. I was hoping the rope would hold and keep it from blowing away. I put my head down and closed my eyes for a while; then I looked up again only to see that it was filling up with water, and the next time I looked, I could only see the top edges swaying back and forth with the waves.

It took a long time for the storm to pass, but finally when it was over, we carefully worked our way out through the branches only to find our dugout floating underwater. That storm sure left us in a fix. Suddenly, I remembered the paddles. We didn't think to take them with us when we climbed into the mangroves. We also left the fish we caught that day and the poles. I looked around and saw that Nakee had found one of the paddles in the water caught under some branches. It was a good thing the wind was blowing the waves toward our little island. At least it kept one paddle from blowing out to sea and maybe the other was nearby too. We looked around but couldn't find it. We couldn't find the fishing poles either. We needed that other paddle, but it was getting late and we had to get the water out of the dugout; but with no beach, there no way for us to empty it before dark. Nakee was sitting on a mangrove branch watching me. I knew he was expecting me to solve this situation. I just stood there holding the rope in one hand and the paddle in the other, and with the water up to my waist, I couldn't think of what to do next.

Earlier in the day we ate the fry bread we brought with us, and now the sun was going down and we had no fire and no food. The sky had cleared and the wind was calm, but the skeeters had started biting real bad. It would be dark soon, so we climbed back into the mangroves to find a good spot to settle in for the night. We tried to get some sleep, but instead we spent all night slapping the skeeters off us. How those skeeters didn't wind up on the other side of the ocean with all that wind I'll never understand.

Morning finally came, and the sun was sending a bit of light out across the sky. We were itching and scratching our skeeter bites so much that we couldn't wait to get out of that place to get away from them. It was hard to see where to step with the branches casting shadows everywhere, but we slowly managed to work our way out of the mangroves. To our surprise the tide had gone out and the dugout was full of water laying high and dry on the sand. We quickly started scooping water out with our hands, but it took a long time before it was just half-empty. The tide started coming in enough to make it float up off the sand, and the more water we scooped out, the higher it floated. We spent most of the morning emptying that thing until finally there was barely any water left. The sun would finish drying it out, and we were eager to be on our way. We looked around again for the other paddle, but it must have gotten blown out to sea because it was nowhere to be found, but at least we had one paddle to help us get away from that island. I hadn't thought of my hatchet with everything else that was going on, so when I suddenly remembered, I reached for it quick and to my relief it was still hanging around my waist real tight.

We couldn't be too far from the village, so I looked around to see if I could see anything familiar, but I couldn't. We needed to go toward where the sun had risen in the east or to the north, so we got in the dugout and pushed off. I sat in the back and began to paddle, staying real close to the mangroves still hoping to find the lost paddle. Nakee was pulling the branches in the front of him and pushing them away as we passed. We worked our way around the small island, and when we got to the other side we stopped and saw that we had to cross some open water to get to where I thought we needed to go. I knew Tayki was going to be real mad at me, but we were both anxious to get back to the chikee to eat and put some ointment on our skeeter bites. The water was calm, so I was sure it would be easy to paddle across. We were about halfway there, and I kept paddling, but we weren't getting anywhere. Even though the tide was coming in and the water was calm, the current was taking us out farther away from what at that moment seemed to be all those safe little islands. Nakee was hanging over the front of the dugout helping paddle with his hands. He was yelling for me to paddle harder, and I was starting to get real worried. No matter how hard I paddled we kept getting pushed farther and farther out to sea.

.

12

It was midafternoon, and my arms couldn't paddle anymore. We were just floating in the Gulf where we could see land in the distance toward the east and nothing but water everywhere else. We tried paddling from time to time during the day, but mostly we floated around, just laying there in the hot sun. A few dark clouds rolled over us in the late afternoon but didn't give us any rain; then the sun started drifting down in front of us. Once it touched the horizon that ball of flames went down fast, lighting up the sky with every color you could think of. It was a beautiful sight that kept our minds off our bad situation only for a few moments till it was all gone. We were left in the dark real hungry, scared, and tired from not getting any sleep the night before. I held Nakee close to me as we lay in the bottom of the dugout that rocked so gently in the water, and we both fell fast asleep.

It was late in the morning when we woke up with the heat of the sun burning down on us. I looked around and could still see land far away on the horizon, and my arms had rested, so I started to paddle. I didn't have much strength, and I was so hot and thirsty and I needed to eat. Nakee tried to paddle for a while, but he was too weak to do any good, so I told him to stop and save his strength. I kept splashing seawater on us to cool us off, but we needed water to drink. Our skin was red and burning from the sun. The salt water stung all the sores from the skeeter bites we scratched so much that night we slept in the mangroves. We needed fresh water real bad. We also needed food.

Later in the day as we laid on the bottom of the dugout, the rain clouds started rolling in and the air got cooler. I was afraid we were in for another bad storm that would put us underwater, but instead the clouds brought us some relief with a soft breeze and quick shower. We caught the rain in our hands and drank as much as we could, but it ended too soon to quench our thirst. The rain rinsed some of the salt off our skin, and that made us feel better, but we were hungrier than ever.

The coolness of the rain gave us enough energy to start paddling again, but not for long, and after a long day the sun was going down again. We were about to spend another night floating in the sea. We were scared and hungry. Our bellies were hurting so bad it was hard to sleep. With our skin burning and our bellies hurting we spent the night in agony just hoping it would be over soon. Morning came, and the sun started to rise. There wasn't a cloud anywhere in the sky. It was going to be another hot, scorching day. I lifted my head above the edge of the dugout to see how far we were from the land. I was hoping to have drifted closer during the night. I didn't see land on that side, so I pushed myself up, looked all around, and got real scared.

Nakee managed to sit up, and in a raspy voice he said, "Where are we? I don't see land no more."

He laid back down, curled his body up, and softly started crying. "I want Momma, my belly hurts, I wanna go home."

I was feeling real bad too; the pain in my belly was too much to bear. "Are we gonna die out here?" I thought to myself. I laid back down and pulled my knees up tight against my chest.

My belly hurt real bad, and my skin was on fire. I started to think that if I died first Nakee would be out here all alone, so I decided that it would be best if he died first. I couldn't bear thinking of all that, and tears started running down my cheeks.

We laid there in the bottom of the dugout drifting out to sea for a long time. The pain on our skin and in our bellies was just too much to take. The sun was high in the sky, but I knew Nakee wasn't dead yet because, like mine, his throat was so dry I could hear him wheezing with every breath he took. I fell asleep for a while but woke up when Nakee started moving around. He sat up and said to me as loud as his throat would let him that he was going home. He tried to stand up, and I was afraid he was going to flip us over. I grabbed hold of him, and he struggled but was too weak to get away. He was saying things that didn't make sense. I could hardly hold on to him, but when he tried to step out of the dugout I pulled real hard and he fell down next to me. I felt his head bump against the wood as I passed out, and that was all I could remember.

I don't know how much time passed, but as I struggled to open my eyes, I could only see my knees as I held them close to my face to try to ease the pain in my belly. My skin burned so much with the heat of the sun blazing down on me, and I knew I probably wouldn't survive another day in such misery. I was remembering how we had drifted away from land and wound up in the vastness of the open sea. My yearning for water was so fierce I believed it wasn't gonna be long before my innards were gonna be sizzlin' right out of me like those white stringy things that come outta eggs when you boil them too long. I remembered forgetting eggs boiling over the fire once, and Pa was mad at me for doing so because he liked his eggs boiled soft. I lay dying in that cypress dugout, floating aimlessly in so much water with not a breath for a breeze, and I was thinking about what I'd give to eat those boiled eggs right then.

I figured it must have been the evil spirits causing our misery. My only other thought was I'd never see Nakee again and I didn't have a chance to say a proper goodbye. Then my eyes defiantly closed while I drifted off to places beyond my thoughts.

Nakee had not been right in the head from the heat of the sun and lack of water. His mind was telling him to walk back to the safety of the chikee where we slept safely so many nights ago. Fear was growing inside him, making him fight with me. I did all I could to keep him from jumping into the depths of the sea to never appear again.

13

I thought I was dreaming when I heard seagulls squawking overhead; then voices in the distance told me that my swollen, blurred eyes needed to open. I lifted my head slowly. The brightness of the sun didn't keep my squinting eyes from seeing Nakee's lifeless body next to me having water splashed on his face; then in one swoop a splash of that cool, fresh water came my way with a stinging pain and relief in one instant. Relief from enduring the torture of the heat, hunger, and thirst for what seemed like weeks and not just a couple of days. I was relieved to know that when Nakee hit his head, he passed out before having a chance to sink to the bottom of the sea.

"C'mon, boys, wake up," I heard a faraway voice say. Before I could lift my heavy eyelids again, my mind floated to that faraway place where I spent lazy days fishing in the Glades with Nakee when the native boys weren't giving us trouble. Tayki was probably real worried. She trusted me to care for her only child and I failed.

The creaking of the timbers grew from a distant annoyance to a real disturbance to my thoughts; my mind was slowly gaining its presence and I was waking up. I opened my eyes and felt my body swaying in a hammock. I heard something dragging on the roof above me; then it stopped with a hard snap that caught my attention. I was on a boat. The deck was above me and that hard snap was the sail.

I laid there real confused as to how I came to be on that boat and what was happening; then my mind took a quick turn back to Nakee. Where was he?

"Nakeeeee!" I tried yelling as loud as my dried-up throat would let me.

Too weak to scramble out of the swaying hammock that like a cradle held me in such safety, I leaned over and rolled out. Right then a wave hit the boat, causing my limp body to fly forward into the bulkhead then drop to the floor. Every part of my body hurt. I couldn't move.

"Nakee, Nakeeee," I tried yelling again, but I think I made no sound.

I was painfully managing to pick myself up after laying there a bit. It wasn't until my eyes were looking straight down at the floor in the dim light when for the first time I noticed the familiar salty fish smell in the air.

"Town?" I whispered, trying to get my thoughts together.

"Pa?" I said, not remembering his fate a couple of years back.

I looked around the floor then looked up to see a hammock almost above me. With nothing else to reach for, I grabbed it to steady my balance as I worked my way to standing up a bit. Pulling myself up some more, my eyes rose over the top edge of the hammock and I came face-to-face with a creature I'd never seen before. This creature had a nose that was about to fall off its face if one more piece of skin let loose and a mouth with lips that looked like they were gonna bust wide open any second. There were no eyes that I could see, just long swollen slits where there should've been eyes, and its skin was bubbling and oozing real bad. I took all that in with just one glance while letting loose of that hammock, and with all the strength running through my entire body, I scrambled to the other side of the cabin, lifting my arm over my face so as not to see if that creature was gonna come after me. It didn't. No, it didn't come after me. It just laid there quietly.

"It's dead!" I thought to myself. No, they'd done thrown something that ugly overboard if it was dead.

All was still for a moment, but before long that thing began to wheeze so pitiful like. I slowly lowered my arm so my eyes could peek over my elbow at that thing, and that's when I saw in the dim light that my arm too was bubbling and oozing much like that wheezing thing laying in that hammock. I reached up to my face only to feel my lips, and like that creature's, they were about to bust wide open. My nose, it too, with all its skin peeling off, was about to fall off my face. "Nakee!" I cried as I looked up; then I began crawling slowly toward the hammock. I reached high to pull myself up again and slowly peeked over the edge of the hammock and through my own slit eyes was able to only stare at him. Just then, I was coming to my senses, remembering the days in the dugout with the sun blazing down and cooking us both well done. That creature was Nakee! I reached over to grab his shoulder and shook him some.

"Nakee," I whispered. "Nakee, wake up."

Just then the light coming from the companionway was blocked to where I couldn't see Nakee anymore. There was a shadow of a man resting down on his face.

"Who are you?" I asked defensively, barely holding myself up in front of Nakee's hammock.

As weak as I was, I was gonna protect Nakee with all I had left in me.

"I'm Captain O'Keef, and you're aboard the Bonnie Sue," the man said. "Who are you?"

"I'm Willie. I'm Willie Sawgrass, sir," I answered, trying to sound brave.

"Well, Willie Sawgrass, it looked like you were in quite a predicament. It's a miracle you're still alive," he said as he walked over to me.

"Yes sir, Captain, sir, we sure was lucky 'n I thank ya much, sir," I answered softly. "Is he gonna be all right?" I asked, looking back at Nakee. By then I could hardly hold myself up, so I let myself down slowly and collapsed onto the floor; then I let go of the hammock and my hand fell down beside me. I could barely hold back my tears.

"I hope so. If we can get enough water and some food in him soon, he might be OK," the captain said.

I looked up at Captain O'Keef and asked, "Sir, my belly hurts real bad. Can I get some food too?"

"Don't worry. We're gonna get lots of food in you too," he said as he reached down and took my hand to pull me up gently; then he helped me take a couple of steps and sat me down in the hammock. He put some water in a cup for me and walked away. I was left sitting in the hammock, looking over at Nakee and just hoping he was gonna get better soon; then I quickly drank all the water in the cup.

By then it was late in the afternoon and I felt the cool breeze coming through the front hatch. I could tell we were in for some rain.

There was a lot of banging on deck, and Captain O'Keef hollered over to me that the crew was battening down the hatches because the rain was coming. I couldn't see what the captain was doing on the other side of the cabin, but soon enough he came around and offered me bread and cheese. He also gave me smoked fish and beans, but it was too salty for me to eat right then. He poured me some more water and told me to eat as much as I wanted; then he quickly went up on deck. I ate real slow for a long time until my belly started feeling better. The bread hurt my throat, but it was good to get food in my belly. I was still real worried about Nakee.

The men above were yelling, and the boat started rocking hard. The waves were real big, and I was glad we weren't in the dugout anymore. We'd be dead for sure by now. I hoped they left it to sink deep into the sea because I never wanted to see it ever again.

As weak as I was, I managed to get my legs up from the floor into my hammock. I laid there swaying back and forth with the waves, watching Nakee sway in the other hammock. It was good to know that he was in there real good and safe and being looked after by someone who could help him.

I woke up to the sound of chains hitting the boat. I knew I had slept a long time because everything was calm and it was getting dark. One of the men above yelled that the anchor was set for the night. The lanterns were lit, and I could see Captain O'Keef gently sitting Nakee up in his hammock. He was trying to feed him and make him drink some water. Nakee didn't look too good, so I asked the captain how he was doing.

"I don't know yet, Willie, but we'll do the best we can," the captain said.

I got up, but I was so weak I could barely make my way to them. I sat next to Nakee as the captain held him up, and I started stroking his hair away from his eyes. I wanted so bad to see those big blue eyes looking back at me.

"His name is Nakee," I said to the captain softly.

Then I looked at the captain and said, "He's my brother."

He looked at me questioningly but didn't say anything more. He got Nakee to swallow water a couple more times then laid him back down gently. I laid down next to Nakee, and we both slept till morning.

14

"Oooh . . . my belly hurts," I heard a raspy voice say softly, and he started moaning in pain. It woke me up real quick, and with all I had in me, I tried yelling for Captain O'Keef.

A man named Slate was below and heard me. He glanced over at us then yelled up at the captain to come quick. "I think the boy's finally waking up!" he yelled.

Slate pulled me up first; then he helped Nakee sit up. He reached for cheese and a cup of water to give to Nakee, and by then Captain O'Keef was coming down to see what was going on.

"Well, this is good news," the captain said, smiling as he saw Nakee take a sip of water.

He reached over and opened Nakee's eyes a little to look at them. Then the captain told Slate to make sure Nakee got lots of food and water in him during the next few days and to keep us both resting as much as possible. The captain went back up on deck.

Nakee's eyes weren't opening real well on their own, and I didn't know if he could see me so I just stroked his hair gently.

"Nakee? Can you hear me?" I said to him slowly. "This is Willie. I'm right here, I'm right next to you," I assured him.

He opened his eyes a little more, and the corners of his mouth went up smiling a little; then his eyes closed. He took a couple more little bites of cheese then pushed it away.

"You need to eat, Nakee. Please? You need to get strong again," I said.

I told him how brave he was and how much I needed him. I also told him how sorry I was to have put him through this; after all, it was my fault he was suffering so much. Then, the man named Slate laid him back down on the hammock and I started talking to him about all the things we use to do when we lived in the village. I talked to him for a long time; then I drank more water and tried to eat. I had to get strong so I could help Nakee get better.

A couple of days later, Nakee was eating and drinking real well, and even though I was feeling better too, Captain O'Keef still made both of us rest a lot. Our skin was a lot darker than usual, and it was peeling real bad but wasn't burning anymore. We were on a big fishing schooner called the *Bonnie Sue* heading north from Key West. The captain's crew was real nice except for Cal; he didn't talk to us much. I had a bad feeling about the man after he walked by me one time and pushed me out of the way. He had a mean way of looking at everyone and mostly kept to himself.

One night when Nakee and me were sitting on deck with the captain I wanted to ask him about that man. "I'm real sorry to tell ya, Captain, but I don't like that man named Cal," I whispered.

"Me, too. He's mean," Nakee said.

I turned quickly and glared at Nakee. "Shhh, be quiet," I said sternly.

Captain O'Keef smiled at us and said it was just the way he was. "I know he's pretty rough, but he's a hard worker and he's real strong. This is a big boat; I need strong men to work it."

I liked the captain and quickly said to him, "I'm strong, Captain O'Keef. I can help you." I looked at Nakee and back to the captain then added, "We can both help you."

"Now wait a minute," the captain said, "don't you have a home to go to?"

I thought about Tayki; then I looked over at Nakee.

"We ain't got no home," said Nakee, looking real sad.

I wondered why Nakee said that. He must have liked being on that boat as much as me, and we both liked Captain O'Keef. Nakee and me never had a real pa or any man to teach us how to do man things, so I went along and agreed with Nakee.

"Nakee's right, sir, we don't have a home," I lied. "My momma and my pa are dead and Nakee's from the Indian village and they call him nonhuman 'cause he's half-white so they don't want him there and we wanna stay with you!" I explained real fast before I ran out of breath.

"Can we stay with you, Captain O'Keef?" Nakee asked real pitiful like, and we both looked at the captain, eagerly waiting for an answer.

"Well," said Captain O'Keef while rubbing that short, well-trimmed beard of his. "Of course, I could use a couple more deck-hands, but first you're going to have to show me how strong you are; then, I'll have to think about it," he said.

Nakee and me quick took off our shirts and started showing off our muscles to him. We were real strong.

.

15

The next day we woke up anxious, wanting to know if Captain O'Keef had thought about keeping us on as deckhands. We scrambled up on deck quickly and ran to him. The sails were up and the captain was holding the ship's wheel. We were real excited, jumping around him, asking if he had thought about it and if we were gonna stay with him.

Captain O'Keef waited patiently for us to settle down. "What about school?" he asked.

"What?" I yelled in a shocked and surprised voice as my bouncing around quickly came to a sudden halt.

I was never so surprised at any question in my life until then. Captain O'Keef wasn't one of them church ladies from town. What would he be asking us about school for?

"School? What do you mean, school?"

"Don't you have to go to school?" he asked, calmly looking ahead toward the bow of the boat.

"For an education?" I asked with my voice trailing up loudly. "No sir! We don't need no schoolin'!" I said defiantly.

"No we don't!" said Nakee; then he asked, "What's education?"

Captain O'Keef yelled over to Cal and told him we were gonna be heading in and he needed to get the dock lines out soon. He told us to go find something to do, that we were going to talk about this later, so Nakee and me walked away.

With all the excitement, I hadn't notice we were heading in toward land north of the big harbor. I started getting worried that Captain O'Keef was going in to drop us off before heading out to sea again.

"I don't wanna go back," Nakee said, looking back at me as I followed him, giving him little pushes forward toward the companionway. I wanted him to go below quick so we could talk about what to do.

We thought about going back to the village, but our minds were made up. We wanted to stay with Captain O'Keef. I was determined we were gonna stay on the *Bonnie Sue* and be fisherman deckhands.

Slate leaned into the companionway and told us we were going to the fish house then head over to a shipyard for a couple of days to do some maintenance on the *Bonnie Sue*. As we went in the inlet we saw lots of fishing boats and some of them had nets out. Captain O'Keef's boat was big but not as big as those ships used for carrying phosphate. Phosphate, Slate said, is something from the ground that helps plants in the garden grow if you sprinkled it on them. Those ships were so big you could put the whole chikee village on just one of them.

After going around the point and into the back bay to the fish house to sell our catch, we finally reached the shipyard. Nakee and me tried to help tie the boat up, but everyone told us we were in the way, so we sat on a deck box to watch and wait for them to finish. Captain O'Keef got off the boat and we watched as he walked down the dock to a little house at the end.

"Where's he going?" I shouted.

Slate said it was the dockmaster's house. The dockmaster was the man in charge of all the boats that came in for repairs, and past his house a ways was the fish house. In town, back home, we didn't have a dockmaster. Everyone just kinda took care of themselves, and the water was too shallow for big boats to come in. I saw Captain O'Keef walking back on the dock toward us with two men.

"Them two men's comin' for us," I whispered to Nakee.

"I don't wanna go," he said sadly.

"We ain't going nowhere," I whispered, desperately thinking of what to do.

I told Nakee to hide in a dory till the men left, so we climbed in and waited. I was peeking out from under the canvas cover when I saw Cal walking toward the plank carrying a bag over his shoulder; then I saw my hatchet hanging from the bag.

"Whatcha doing with my hatchet?" I yelled at him as I jumped out of the dory.

I ran to him with my hand balled up in a fist. I got in front of him and looked right in his eyes.

"That's my hatchet! You give it back to me! It's mine!" I said, gritting my teeth.

Nakee ran over and yelled "Yeah, that's Willie's hatchet, give it back!" Then he kicked Cal in the shin.

Right then Cal quickly flung his hand out, hitting Nakee in the head and sending him sideways to the ground.

Captain O'Keef came over real quick and grabbed me around my waist just as I was ready to jump on Cal.

"He stole my hatchet! That's mine! Tell him to give it back, it's mine!" I yelled, throwing my fists in the air and kicking my legs wildly at Cal. I was twisting my body violently, trying to get loose from the captain's grip, but he held on tight.

Captain O'Keef told Cal not to ever lay a hand on Nakee, or me, again. I could tell by his voice that he was angry; then he asked Cal where he got the hatchet.

"Got it from the dugout when we rescued these sea rats. They was about gone anyway and I didn't think they'd need it," Cal said with his evil voice making me even madder than I already was.

"Give it back to the boy," Captain O'Keef ordered. "If you touch one of them again, you'll be answering to me."

Cal handed it over and I yanked it from his hand quickly; then I squirmed out of the captain's hold and stomped away with Nakee following loyally behind me.

"You best keep it in a safe place from now on," Cal yelled over at me, and he laughed as he walked down the plank.

I had not thought about my hatchet since before we got rescued and was gonna keep it with me always from then on. I tied a piece of rope around my waist and tucked it in by my side.

To my relief, the two men had come to help the crew do some repairs to the boat. They weren't here to take us away. Captain O'Keef was real busy, so Nakee and me waited the rest of the day before we could talk to him. Finally, it was late afternoon and everyone was getting ready to leave the boat. They were going somewhere called Millie's to get food and drinks. Captain O'Keef told us to go with him.

We walked from the boatyard down a sandy road where we could hear lots of strange loud noises. I asked Captain O'Keef what it was. I'd never heard noises like that before; then suddenly along with a chuggin' noise came two loud whistles, and that turned into a loud, hissing screech.

The captain said, "That's a train."

"It's so loud. What's it for?" I asked.

Nakee shouted looking back at the captain, "What's a train?"

"You'll see," he answered.

We reached a sharp bend in the road and walked around several houses to a big building called the "train station." That's when I saw it. It was a train right in front of us! Nakee and me never saw a train before, and it was some sight. There were big metal boxes with wheels and windows, and there were people in those boxes. The front one, Captain O'Keef said, was called the engine. It was a place for a captain to drive that thing. There were also automobiles. We'd never seen an automobile in real life and there they were, a bunch of them sitting side by side next to the station. There was a man driving one, and it was making lots of noise coming down the trail toward us.

Even the church ladies in town dressed in their Sunday best couldn't match up to the fancy-dressed people on the train. Those ladies wore pretty dresses and carried something the captain called parasols. There were lots of seagulls flying around the fishing docks nearby, so I figured the parasols were to keep certain things from falling on their fancy hats. The men too were dressed real nice, wearing black bows around their necks. They were helping the ladies step down the steps of the train. Even the black men carrying people's bags were all dressed up. They had black bows around their necks and wore funny little hats. I just stood there and stared. I'd never seen any place like that in all my life.

Suddenly, from a distance, I heard Nakee call over to me, and I saw him waving at me from the steps of the train. He was getting on. I wanted to get on that thing too. I ran and jumped on the first step where he was standing, and when we looked up to step in, a man blocked the doorway. We politely asked him to excuse us, but the man looked down and told us to get off, that we weren't allowed on the train. We were real disappointed as we backed down off that thing. By then Captain O'Keef had walked over. He grabbed us both by the back of the neck, turned us around, and started guiding us in front of him toward the road.

"Ok, let's go. You've seen enough for now and we have to eat," he said.

To tell you the truth, I was getting hungry, but with all that excitement I had forgot about food.

16

There were lots people eating and drinking at Millie's place. It was a much better place than Jack's back home. I saw Cal sitting alone at a table by the wall. We sat down, and a lady named Millie brought us a pitcher of water and some glasses. The captain ordered turtle soup first; then, he ordered pan-fried snapper, potatoes, and green beans. While we waited, we talked about trains, cars, and far-away places. We got our food and were eating when Captain O'Keef pulled out a little book and a pencil from his pocket and started writing. Nakee and me were quietly eating and curiously watching him.

He looked up at us and asked, "Can you do this?"

"Do what?" I asked.

"Write," he said, pointing at what he had written.

"No, we don't know how to write," I answered.

"What do ya need to know how to write for?" Nakee asked.

"Same reason you need to know how to read," the captain said. "It's a way to communicate your thoughts and ideas."

We were kind of puzzled at what he was getting at, but then he told us that reading and writing was what you learned in school. I started thinking about how the church ladies talked about sending me to school and I didn't even know what school was. All I knew was that Pa always said I didn't need school and, he insisted, I wasn't going to do what the church ladies said.

I listen to Captain O'Keef and started paying attention to how different he was from Pa. Captain O'Keef was real nice and people liked him. He was strong and men respected him, and when Millie brought us our food he said, "Thank you." Pa wasn't like that. I never heard Pa say thank you, and he didn't like anybody and nobody liked him. Pa thought of what was good for just him. I wondered if Pa would have liked Captain O'Keef. Probably not. Then, I figured that Captain O'Keef might not have liked Pa too much either.

"Are you paying attention, Willie?" asked Captain O'Keef, drawing my attention back to what he was saying.

"What?" I said, shaking my head.

"I was telling you what letters are for," he said.

"Huh? Letters, I don't know," I said.

Then Captain O'Keef looked up toward Millie and raised his finger in the air, and she came over. He told her we were done and gave her money; then we headed out the door. We strolled by a big place called a hotel where all the fancy people stayed when they were here visiting; then we passed by the train station. Captain O'Keef asked curiously about my hatchet hanging on my waist. I told him how I came to get my hatchet and that I could show him how to throw it if he wanted me to. He said he'd like that. I saw a log on the side of the road, so I stopped the captain and told him I was gonna hit it right in the middle. I raised my hatchet and threw it, hitting my target. Captain O'Keef was real impressed with my hatchet-throwing skills and said that if I could teach him how to throw a hatchet he would teach us how to read. Not being real sure about that, I was convinced real quick when he said it was the only way we could stay with him.

17

The next morning we got up early. The men were already on deck working. Nakee and me wanted to take another look at the train, but as we walked down the plank, Captain O'Keef shouted for us to stop. He asked where we were going. When we told him, he shook his head and said that we weren't going anywhere. We were going to start learning about letters; then we were going help wash the boat down. He took us below into the main cabin and pulled out a book. I'd never seen any book other than the church ladies' Bible. I told Captain O'Keef that the church ladies wanted me to know what was in that Bible but to me it looked like there was nothing but paper. I also told him that the ladies said there were words in there but they weren't fooling me because I knew books couldn't talk.

"Of course books can't talk," said Captain O'Keef.

"Sure enough," I said.

"But they can tell you stories of faraway places and fill your mind with knowledge," he said.

"What? How do they do that?" I asked, doubting what he was telling me.

"Books do have words, and words are made up of letters, so you have to know how the letters go together to know what they say," Captain O'Keef explained.

He opened the book and pointed to all the words, but they didn't make sense to me. Then he closed the book and showed us the cover.

"*Moby Dick*," said Captain O'Keef, pointing to the letters.

"This book will take you out to sea on an adventure with Captain Ahab in search of a great white whale called Moby Dick," he told us.

Then Captain O'Keef took out his pencil and showed Nakee and me the letters c-a-t. Those were the first letters we learned, and that was the beginning of our education. Nakee and me spent every morning learning about letters, and soon we learned how to put three letters together to make words. During the day we helped cut bait for the longlines, and when the fish came in, we'd throw them in the hold where they were kept cold with ice. Every night with the candles lit below deck, Captain O'Keef read to us about Captain Ahab and that whale called Moby Dick. It was real exciting, and sometimes Captain O'Keef would find words we learned and he would help us read them.

We went offshore to fish for a few days at a time. Then we'd head in to unload our catch at the fish house. We spent many months doing this until one day when the weather started cooling off Captain O'Keef said we had to start thinking about heading south soon. He said we were going to fish the waters off Key West.

It was early in the morning when after loading the boat with provisions and ice we were on our way with full sails up. We were heading south with the cool November breeze, and it would be a couple of hours yet before the sun would come up.

The water wasn't too rough, and we were anticipating an uneventful day. The air was dry and the breeze was cool, but that didn't fool me none. I knew the sun would be blazing down on us soon enough as it didn't take long for that Florida sun to heat up the day even in the wintertime. The crew and Nakee had settled down below for some extra sleep before sunup, but as always, I stayed by the helm to keep the captain company as we navigated our way down the coast. Captain O'Keef said it would take most of the day before we'd reach the Marquesas to anchor for the night; then we were going to fish the next day before heading into Key West.

The morning passed and the sun was up, over the horizon. We had good weather, and the wind was moving us right along when we saw a boat in the distance to the south. We approached with caution, and as we got closer we heard cows bellowing. It was a cattle boat that had run up on some big coral heads. The bow hit the coral heads during the early morning hours and was sinking. Most of the cattle were swimming around the boat as they had been driven overboard by the crew to lighten the load. We could hear men shouting while working the pumps as hard as they could. They couldn't keep up with the amount of water coming in and were losing the battle to keep the stern from sinking.

Captain O'Keef yelled for all hands on deck; then we lowered the sails and eased up close to them. We saw the look of desperation on their faces at first then relief as they looked over at us.

"We're here to help!" shouted Captain O'Keef. "It's pretty shallow, and from here we can see when the stern goes down it'll hit the bottom, but the bow will probably still be sitting high enough on the coral for a while."

The men were relieved to know they could take a minute to catch their breath but desperately wanted to save the cattle.

Cows are good swimmers, but they had been swimming for a while and some had gone under while others were bumping against the boat. After a little while the stern of the boat sank, and when the keel hit bottom, it listed a little. The cows were bellowing and snorting, desperately pawing at the deck and trying to board from the stern, which for a moment was steady on the bottom. As their hooves beat against the deck they slowly began sliding sideways.

"It's gonna roll over!" one of the men yelled. Captain O'Keef shouted for us to put the dories in the water and throw anchors out to steady the sinking boat. It looked like the boat was going to turn on its side but held steady after the anchors were out. As it listed, more cows slid over the side rail on the stern; then they all turned and started swimming toward us.

Captain O'Keef commanded loudly, "Swing the boom out and start hoisting some of those cows on board!"

Then he yelled, "Try to get the younger ones!"

He knew we couldn't load them all and the smaller they were, the more we could save. Just at that moment one of the men from the other boat jumped into the water. He grabbed the end of a rope from our boat and swam under a cow. Then he came up on the other side of it, and with the rope in hand, he tied it around the cow to hoist it up. As we brought it on board the cattle in the water turned toward the man and wedged him against our boat. With the mass of cattle around him, his only choice was to go underwater, but while not able to escape the hooves frantically kicking him around, he met his fate and we never saw him again.

The cows turned again this time toward the sinking boat. They began swimming away from us as we tried to lasso them to pull them in and get them on board. Then Nakee yelled, "Let's use the net!" I looked at Captain O'Keef; then Nakee and I ran to get a big mullet net we had on board. We tied one end of the net on the end of the boom and the other around a winch while the rest hung in the water. Just then a cow swam over the net.

"We got one! Pull!" I yelled.

"Pull it in!" the captain ordered.

Nakee and I began turning the winch handle, and when Slate came over to help, I ran to help the captain haul in the boom. The young cow looked real scared hanging over the water with its eyes wide open. After we pulled him in and untangled him from the net he didn't want to move; he just laid there.

"Push! Get him off the net!" Nakee yelled.

"I'll winch the net out from under him!" I shouted.

I ran back to the winch and started turning the handle. The net slid across the deck with the cow on it until it was right next to me.

"Get off!" I screamed as I kicked that cow on its side. It quickly jumped up and ran across the deck.

We threw the net overboard again hoping to snag another one, but by then they were out of reach and heading toward the sinking boat. The bow of that boat was sliding down a little, and with the stern further underwater it allowed the cows to climb on board. The cows were louder than ever. Little did they know they would be back in the water real soon again if we couldn't get to them on board the *Bonnie Sue*.

"Get the plank!" the captain ordered.

We maneuvered the *Bonnie Sue* as close to the sinking boat as we could and connected the two boats with a plank. The cows started running across the plank, one after another coming toward us, while others unsuccessfully tried jumping across.

"Stop them! Stop them! There's too many!" Nakee screamed as he was scrambling to get out of their way.

BANG! A shot rang out.

A cow suddenly stopped and fell into the water. I looked over and saw Captain O'Keef holding a gun in his hand. Then shot after shot rang out, clearing the plank so we could remove it.

"We're loaded! We can't take anymore!" the captain yelled.

I looked over at Nakee, understanding what had to be done. No matter how grim the task was, we couldn't leave the cows in the middle of the ocean to suffer. Captain O'Keef had to shoot them, but he left some small ones for the men to rescue. We managed to snag some dead cows with the grappling hook then scooped them

out of the water with the net, but soon the sharks came to feed on the rest. The two men from the cattle boat boarded the *Bonnie Sue* and took care of the live cows. They laid them on the deck and tied their hooves together so they couldn't get up.

It was midafternoon when the situation was finally under control. We had a heavy load, so it was fortunate we didn't have any fish on board yet. There were sixteen heifers, two young bulls, and eleven calves laying on deck with their hooves tied. The men from the other boat went back to get their things and bring over some feed and hay then went back again to get a few extra barrels of fresh water for the cows while Nakee and me cleaned the decks. The cows sure made a mess pooping and slobbering all over the place. We finally weighed anchor and continued heading south while those men skinned and butchered the six dead cows so they could carry them below to put them in the fish hold on ice. The live cows were going to have to stay tied up until we reached land.

18

We anchored off Cape Sable for the night, and the two men from the other boat properly introduced themselves as Sam and Frank. Captain O'Keef welcomed them on board. We had not eaten yet as we were not prepared for the events of that day, so we were all real hungry. Sam said he had separated some beef hearts to cook up for dinner. He cut up some potatoes, and Nakee and I were given the task of skewering it all together to lay them on the griddle to cook while beans boiled up in a pot hanging over the fire.

During dinner Cal sat quietly in a corner while Sam and Frank told us the story of what happened that day. They said, the captain of the cattle boat and the wealthy rancher who owned the herd had perished along with two other crewmen when they hit the coral. The sun was just high enough to make the sky glow, and they were underway heading south. They told us that two crewmen must have been standing on the bow smoking their first cigarette of the day when the boat came to a hard and sudden stop. The jolt sent them over the bow into the dark water. The cattle were corralled on the back deck, and when they slid forward they broke the barrier that contained them. The captain and the rancher were caught between the cows and the helm where they stood. They did not survive the weight of the cattle against them and the trampling of their hooves.

They told us that they were sleeping below when they were jolted awake by that sudden stop. They ran up on deck and heard the men overboard calling for help. By then the cattle were loose and stumbling around on deck. It was just before daybreak, so it was still dark. Sam and Frank fought their way through the cattle and scrambled to get the lifeboat in the water. They managed to get it over the side, but it quickly sank. A loading boom had slammed into it, splintering some of the planking on the side. The morning was cool, so the two men who fell in the water were fully clothed to stay warm, and they had shoes on, making it difficult for them to swim. The current was just strong enough to keep them from reaching the sinking boat as they desperately tried swimming toward it. Sam and Frank said they threw the life ring out many times to save them but couldn't; the men drifted farther and farther away until they were too far to reach. The light coming over the horizon was casting a shimmering glow on the water, and the bobbing heads of the men could not be seen among the shadows of the small, choppy waves. Before long their voices faded away until all that could be heard was the slapping of the water against the hull of the boat and bellows and hooves of the cattle shifting around on deck. They could not save those men and immediately took on the task of saving their own lives.

The wealthy rancher had kept the herd isolated just south of the harbor for quite some time, so it had not been exposed to the deadly tick fever that caused government officials to eradicate so many herds to the north. These weren't regular scrub cows; they were crossed with a much preferred Brahma breed, Sam and Frank told the captain. They said it was a good healthy herd that had been dipped many times over the past few months, as a precaution to the tick fever disease. They needed them to be healthy before loading them up for the trip to Cuba to sell. The rancher who owned the herd had made a deal with a Cuban rancher and was headed there to deliver them for a good price when the accident happened.

Captain O'Keef documented all that the men told us so he could give it to the authorities when we got back; then he and the crew decided that what was left of the herd belonged to us now and we were going to make the delivery as planned. He said the cows could bring us more money than fish. Our plans changed, and the cows were going to be with us for the night and most of the next couple of days because we were going to Cuba.

19

The next day our first duty was to water and feed the animals. Then, following the captain's orders, Nakee and me went below to do schoolwork for a couple of hours. After that we tended to the cows again. We washed the decks throughout the rest of the day. The *Bonnie Sue* headed southwest, and that cool northwest wind was pushing us along at a pretty good clip considering we had such a heavy load. It would still take a full day of sailing before we could drop anchor for the night just offshore of the main island of the Marquesas.

In early afternoon while standing on the bow, I looked off to the west. I saw a small speck in the horizon . . . then it was gone . . . then I saw it again for a while . . . then it turned away again. I thought my eyes were playing tricks on me, but I was sure it was a boat and I wondered why it kept turning back. We were use to seeing boats at sea now and again, but this one was different. Nakee was on the other side giving cows water, and I was trying to move one of the calves that was wedged in tight between two deck boxes.

"Nakee!" I called over at him.

The animals were restless and bellowing a little, so when I called out to him again he heard me and managed to stumble around some cows to reach me.

"What do you want?" he said.

"Quick! Come here!" I yelled at him.

I pointed to the west and said, "Go up the rigging and look that way to see if you can see another boat! Hurry!"

Nakee quickly handed me the bucket he had in his hand; then he reached for a rope, climbed onto the rail, and went halfway up the shroud. He pointed off into the distance, but I was too low standing on the deck and couldn't see anything. The noise from the wind and animals kept me from hearing what Nakee was saying, but I could tell that he was looking at something far away. The sails were up, and nobody saw him up in the rigging. When he came down he told me there was a boat just over the horizon. I was curious as to why that boat would have come within view of us then turn back. I kept watch and saw it again later in the day do the same thing; then I didn't see it again until early evening and it did the same thing.

We finally saw the island where we planned to spend the night. There was a cove on the leeward side where we set the anchor. It had been a long day and we were anxious for something to eat, so after we wrapped all the sails and got everything shipshape we settled down to fix dinner before the sun set. I was thinking about that boat but then turned my attention to dinner. It was good to have something other than the usual fish to eat. The beef hearts, potatoes, and beans were just as good the second night as the first, and we all enjoyed every bit of it.

After dinner Captain O'Keef pulled out a book. We had enjoyed listening to him read to us about Captain Ahab's adventures with Moby Dick. It was a good book, and we were real glad to see that he was going to start reading another one.

The sun sets early during the winter months, so Captain O'Keef had plenty of time to read before it would be time for us to sleep. It was a comfortably cool evening, so after cleaning up our dinner plates we lit the lanterns and settled in below.

"What's this book called?" Nakee asked.

"This book is called *The Red Badge of Courage*," the captain said. "It's a story about Henry Fleming, an eighteen-year-old private in the United States Army."

The weather outside was calm and our bellies were full. We listened to Captain O'Keef read to us for a long time until finally, his eyes were getting heavy and he stopped. Then, he got up and said that he would have to continue the story another time. It was getting late and we all needed to get to sleep. Everyone got into their hammocks, and the lanterns were snuffed. We had to get up real early to make the crossing.

I was still awake staring into the darkness of the cabin. I could hear the shifting of cows on deck and a bellow now and then. I knew that Nakee was asleep by the steadiness of his breathing, and I could hear a bit of snoring from the men. I couldn't help thinking about Henry Fleming and what life must be like in the army; then finally, as I was drifting off to sleep I heard a thump against the hull. My eyes opened quickly, and in an instant I was wide awake. Not being able to see much in the dark, I laid there and listened carefully.

It wasn't like the shifting noise of the cows or any other sound I was so use to on the boat. I paid close attention then heard it again. I got down quietly from my hammock and grabbed my hatchet from the locker where it was stowed. I crept up the companionway peeking out across the deck. The cold breeze blew across my face, and the moon was out casting shadows from the clouds onto the water, so I couldn't see much.

I quietly climbed on top of the cabin above where Nakee and the men were sleeping, and I laid there on my stomach. I couldn't hear much more than the cows shifting around, so I strained my eyes and looked for anything unusual; then I saw shadows moving around in the water next to the *Bonnie Sue*. There were some men in a small rowboat who under the cover of darkness sneaked up on us. I felt the rowboat hit our hull again.

"Pirates! There's pirates! Pirates! Pirates!" I screamed as loud as I could.

All of a sudden the cows started bellowing and Sam, Frank, and Slate started yelling and scrambling over each other to get on deck. They were climbing over the cows, and I jumped down, clutching my hatchet real tight, and ran behind the foremast. Cal came out of nowhere and was standing next to me for a second; then he was gone. The pirates had already tied their tender up to the *Bonnie Sue* and were unsuccessfully scrambling to get untied. Nakee was real quick to come on deck. He grabbed an oar, put it on the rail, and started swinging it back and forth to keep those pirates from climbing onboard. Then he started hitting the rail with the oar. I ran over to help Nakee when one of the pirates grabbed the other end of the oar and yanked on it. I wrapped my arms around Nakee's waist from behind and held on to him so he wouldn't get pulled overboard.

"Let go of the oar! Let it go!" I screamed at Nakee.

"No! I's gonna get me a pirate!" he yelled back.

"He's gonna pull you over! Let go!" I shouted firmly at him.

I reached around Nakee to grab his hand when my hand instead landed on the big leathery hand gripping the oar. I let go quick and pulled my hand away real fast. I knew that with one more reach, the owner of that leathery hand would grab Nakee and pull him over, so I started swinging at it with the back of my hatchet. I didn't want to accidentally hit Nakee's hand with the blade and maybe slice off his finger, so in the darkness I quickly hammered away at the oar hoping to hit that pirate's hand.

"He's got me! Help me!" Nakee yelled.

Nakee had one foot up on the rail and was pushing it real hard because by then that hand had a hold of Nakee's wrist. I thought I hit that pirate's hand because he let go suddenly and Nakee and me fell backward onto the deck, but when I looked up I could see Slate kneeling next to us rubbing his fist. He must have punched that pirate a good one.

Right then I saw Captain O'Keef bending over the rail, shooting at them. The pirates didn't have a chance of getting the rope untied with bullets flying by, so they cut it but then had to quickly jump into the cold, dark water to get away.

Captain O'Keef was shooting at their tender as it started floating away. He was hoping to put enough holes in it to sink it quickly in the calm water.

Most of the yelling suddenly stopped, and the cows were shifting around on deck, bellowing real loud. We all gathered on the bow with Captain O'Keef and strained to see where the pirates were, but we couldn't see them in the dark. The captain shot one last time toward the island as they had no other choice than to try to swim to it to seek safety. They must have anchored their big boat on the other side of the island and waited till we were sleeping so they could sneak up on us.

"I hope I sank the tender. We don't want them visiting us again," Captain O'Keef yelled over at us, but we could hardly hear him over the bellowing of the cows.

"We showed them pirates, didn't we?" Nakee yelled excitedly.

"That's right and we need to thank Willie for that," Captain O'Keef yelled back at Nakee.

"It was his sharp senses that saved us. Good job, Willie!" Slate yelled.

"Yeah, good job, Willie!" Nakee yelled, sounding real proud of what I had done.

I felt like scolding him for not letting go of that oar, but right then I was a hero and feeling real proud. After thinking about it, I couldn't help but wonder how I could be a hero for something that any one of us could have done? No, I wasn't a hero. I was just the one who happened to be awake and able to sound the alarm.

The cows began calming down, and Captain O'Keef told Slate to keep watch on deck for a couple of hours then to wake Cal up to take the second watch. After that, the captain wanted to be woken to take the early morning watch before heading out for the day.

Captain O'Keef said it would take at least fifteen hours to get to Cuba. The November wind was going to push us along, and even with a heavy load we'd make good time. He wanted to head out before sunup to get across the Florida Straits. We all had to get a good night's sleep, but with the excitement of that evening it was hard to relax.

20

I woke up to the sound of the chain hitting the deck as the men brought the anchor up. It was still dark, but I knew from listening to the activity on deck that it was early morning and time to get underway. The cows were stirring a bit and bellowing softly. I came up the companionway, rubbing the sleepiness out of my eyes, and I could feel the cool, dry air on my face. The lanterns on deck were lit, and I could barely see a thin red line across the horizon where the sun would eventually make its appearance. I could hear the small waves slapping lightly against the hull; then I looked over toward the island and wondered if the pirates made it to shore the night before. Without a tender they'd have a hard time sneaking around some unsuspecting boat anytime soon.

It was still too dark to feed and water the cows, so I went below and lit a lantern to get a pot of coffee started. I knew the men would want it as soon as we got underway. The water was starting to boil when Nakee woke up. I turned to see his head peeking out from the side of the hammock.

"We showed them pirates, didn't we?" Nakee said softly but somewhat excitedly.

I smiled and turned to put the coffee into the boiling water. After a few minutes I heard the sails snap as they filled with air, and I felt the boat heel over a little as we started to move. I grabbed the coffeepot by the handle to keep it from spilling. I kept the pot balanced over the gimbaled stove for a while until it was ready. Then, holding the pot in one hand, I reached over with my other one and grabbed the rail to keep my balance stepping up the companionway.

"Bring them cups," I yelled down at Nakee. "Coffee's ready!" I shouted to the crew.

Nakee came up behind me, and we served out the hot coffee as the sun began lighting up the sky with all its colors; then Nakee and me went below to boil up potatoes for breakfast. Slate came down a while later to help us fix a big pot of scrambled eggs and fried beef.

After breakfast Nakee and me scrubbed the decks. We were sure tired of cleaning up all that cow mess. We were told that we'd get a cut of the money when we sold the cattle in Cuba, so we were excited about that. We never had any money of our own, so while scrubbing all that mess we thought real hard on what we would do with it.

"Let's get a train!" Nakee shouted over to me.

I didn't know much about money, but I thought a train's got to be worth a whole lot more than cows. I was hoping for a whole dollar of that cow money for each of us.

"It's not enough money to buy a train," I told him.

Then I thought of all the people on the train dressed all fancy. I figured if we couldn't buy a train we could surely buy us fancy clothes. I never had store-bought clothes before. I just wore what the church ladies made for me, and mostly my clothes were always dirty and torn. When I went to live at the village, Tayki made me my colorful pants like what the native boys wore.

"Nakee, we's gonna get us store-bought clothes is what we's gonna do!" I said.

I was washing the deck around the cows, and when I emptied the bucket of water near my feet I looked at them for a moment and thought how I never had shoes before. All them fancy people on that train had shiny new shoes on their feet.

"We're going to get us shoes too," I said.

The captain heard us talking and yelled over at us. "I think that's a great idea, Willie. When we get to Cuba I'll take you where you can get a real bath too, with soap. Then we'll get you two some new clothes and new shoes so you can be clean, proper young boys."

I quickly thought of them church ladies always wanting me to be proper and civilized. I never knew what that was, but I was beginning to get the idea.

"Captain? What's civilized mean?" I asked.

"Civilized is the way one lives, using manners, being polite and kind to others. It also means having an education. If one is educated, the rest comes naturally," he explained.

I knew right then that Pa really was uncivilized and I wasn't gonna be like Pa. Maybe the church ladies were right. I was starting to believe that Pa was wrong about a lot of things.

I decided I was going to be educated and civilized like Captain O'Keef, so after I finished swabbing the decks I willingly went below and got a book to read. *Treasure Island* was the book I picked out.

I struggled and barely could read the first couple of pages, but I forced myself until I finally decided that it would be easier for Captain O'Keef to read it to us when we got to Cuba after dinner one night. Maybe he could help me and Nakee read some words.

I went back up on deck and saw Nakee was playing with the cows. The cows, I was sure, were getting real tired of being tied up, and I couldn't wait to reach land to get them off the boat so we wouldn't have to keep feeding and watering them and especially cleaning up after them.

We had been sailing since early morning and fixed a big meal in the late afternoon. The sun was going down, and it wouldn't be long till we'd be sailing in the dark. Slate took the helm, and Cal lit a lantern on the back deck and one in the cabin below. I sat at the table with Captain O'Keef and watched him study the charts. He was writing numbers on a paper and explained that they were latitude and longitude numbers needed to navigate. Someday he was going to teach me how to figure all that out.

21

We sailed for a long time in the dark before we started to see the Havana lights on the horizon. Captain O'Keef didn't want to go much farther. There could be reefs ahead, and we couldn't take a chance of running up on one in the night. We would have to wait till morning to sail into the port of Havana. After lowering the sails we drifted a bit before the anchor caught something solid enough to be set for the night. I stayed up to take the first watch with Slate, but I fell asleep on the deck laying against a comfortably warm cow. When I woke up I thought I was alone, but soon I noticed Cal standing on the back deck smoking a cigarette. I didn't want to strike up any conversation with him, so I went below, climbed into my hammock, and went back to sleep till morning.

"Hey, everybody, the captain says to wake up!" Nakee yelled as he bounced around the cabin, pulling on everyone's hammock.

"We can see Cuba! We's real close! They sure have some big houses in that place!" he shouted.

I could hear everyone moaning as they wanted to be left alone. Captain O'Keef had let us sleep in a bit longer than usual, but it was after daybreak and we needed to start heading into port. While Frank was on watch during the night he peeled a bunch of potatoes to have ready for breakfast, so we boiled them up and fried eggs. We were all in a hurry to eat because we couldn't wait to go ashore.

The cows must have known something was up because they were getting real restless. They'd been tied up for two days and were ready to get off the boat. We had just one small sail up as we went into the channel to the port of Havana. We could see lots of people everywhere. I'd never seen houses so big. I figured families must be real big and they needed big houses to live in. Slate called the big houses buildings. He said Havana was a city and Nakee and me had never been in a city.

As we went in we saw all kinds of boats and ships coming and going, and many were anchored in the harbor. Slate said some of the big ships were for carrying people to faraway places called "New York" and "Europe." There were lots of busy people walking up and down the streets next to the docks. As we approached a dock, I could hear people talking and yelling, but I couldn't understand a word and I knew for sure they weren't Miccosukee. I asked Slate what they were saying, and he said it was something called Spanish. He said it was a language and there were lots of different languages in the world.

"Why don't they all just speak same as us?" I asked Slate.

He didn't answer me. We were getting close to the dock and he had to lower the sail. Captain O'Keef got off, and I saw him walking down the dock with a couple of men. They headed into what looked to be the dockmaster's house. The rest of us stayed on board the *Bonnie Sue* and tidied up the sails and lines; then we began cleaning the boat. The cows were hungry and thirsty and getting real loud, but I knew we'd get them unloaded soon enough.

I was helping Nakee carry a bucket of water over to some cows when I heard the captain's voice. I looked over to see him walking on board with two men dressed up real nice. They started inspecting the cattle, and I could tell they approved of them. I saw the captain shaking his head. One of the men spoke English but not too well. He was talking to the captain in English; then he was talking to the other man in that Spanish language. I could tell he was the man wanting to buy our cows, but Captain O'Keef kept shaking his head; then he turned and walked away from them men.

"Thirty-two!" the man who spoke English yelled out.

Captain O'Keef turned around and smiled; then he walked back toward the two men and they all shook hands. They were writing something on paper; then the captain shouted over to Slate to get the cattle ready to unload. They got up and stomped around all over the deck. A ramp was placed on the side of the *Bonnie Sue*, and the cows were herded down where some men were waiting on horseback to take them away. I thought he must have gotten a whole thirty-two dollars for all those cows. That was a lot of money.

"I'm glad to be rid of them beasts!" I said as the last one was ready to make its way down the ramp.

"What a mess!" Nakee shouted as he looked around.

"That's right and you two are going to clean up this mess to earn your pay," Captain O'Keef said sternly as he walked by.

Nakee looked over at me, and we both started working real hard to clean the cow mess. We had to wash and scrub the wood decks because we were going to get a couple of dollars like the captain promised. A while later all that meat on ice was taken away and we had to clean the ice hold too. We spent all the rest of the day cleaning. We were real tired, so Captain O'Keef suggested we stop because everybody deserved a good meal and a night on the town. He also said we would be getting our new clothes and shoes the next day. That was exciting for me because I'd never had anything new before.

The captain got us a big table at a fancy restaurant, and there were people playing music and dancing. He told us to order anything we wanted. The only eating place I'd ever been to was Millie's place. While we ate, Sam and Frank were talking about checking out something called cantinas; then they were going to buy rum for the trip back. They wanted to load up the *Bonnie Sue* with crates of rum to sell when we got home. They anticipated making lots of money, but Captain O'Keef put a stop to that conversation real quick. He said it was illegal and he didn't want more than a couple of bottles of rum on his boat for the trip back. I didn't know what a cantina was, but I wasn't going to ask because by then Cal seemed annoyed at the captain's remarks about the rum. Suddenly, he threw his napkin on the table and got up. Sam and Frank got up too. They followed Cal over to where the captain was sitting, and Cal put his hand out in front of him with his palm up. Captain O'Keef knew what Cal wanted, so he took money out and carefully held it right next to his pocket so others couldn't see it. He had a fist full of money and counted out several bills for each of them, and they left. Then, he stuffed it back in his pocket and quickly put his finger to his lips and told us not to say anything.

"I's never seen so much money; can I have some?" Nakee quickly said, putting his hand out for the captain to give him some.

It was a good thing the people around us didn't understand English.

I leaned close to the captain and asked, "Where'd ya get all that money?"

"Cows," he answered, frowning at Nakee's hand in front of him.

"Cows? You got all that for them cows?" I said, not knowing how much a cow cost.

"That's right, thirty-two hundred dollars. They weren't scrub cows; they were prime beef cattle worth a lot. That rancher's going to produce a fine herd with those cows," Captain O'Keef explained quietly. Then he changed the subject. "You need to finish eating so we can head back to the boat and finish reading our book. And we need to get some rest so we can buy you boys new clothes tomorrow."

On our way back to the boat there were lots of people laughing and yelling real loud, and there was music and dancing everywhere. Havana sure was a lively place, but for some reason I couldn't help but think about all the cows I saw on my way to the shack when I went to get Pa's hatchet. Then I thought about all the cows we left behind in the water. The sharks must have had the meal of their life eating cows worth so much money.

I turned my attention to Nakee and started laughing. He was running up and down the street in front of us, laughing and dancing like a crazy fool to the music everywhere around us. Slate and Captain O'Keef were walking behind me, having fun watching Nakee dance, and told me to go dance with him. I ran to Nakee and we both started shaking our bodies to the music, and other people danced with us as we went by them. We were having lots of fun, so we took our time getting back to the boat. When we reached the dock Slate went on board with us, and we all listened to the captain read. After a while Slate wanted to go back into town and we were too tired to listen to more of the story, so we climbed into our hammocks and went to sleep.

It was late into night when I woke up to Cal, Sam, and Frank stumbling around and making such a racket on deck. They were yelling for Captain O'Keef.

"Hey, Captain, get up here! We wanna talk to you!" Sam hollered.

"Ya want some rum? C'mon, Captain, come hav'a little drinky with us," Frank said, slurring his words.

"You men better settle down. Sleep it off or get off my boat!" the captain yelled, looking out the companionway.

Those men were drunk and wouldn't let up. They kept yelling nonsense at the captain. Then, I could tell it was Sam that started singing; then Frank joined in. They sang their hearts out about some lady named "Smeralda," and one of them started crying. Then they both started crying and singing at the same time and Cal kept yelling at them to shut their mouths.

"Why's they crying?" Nakee asked, looking at the captain.

"They's drunk!" I said real quick before the captain could answer. "They's drinking rum and rum's got spirits that makes a man not right in the head."

The captain walked by and snapped at us to go back to sleep. We couldn't help but listen to them carry on for a while; then it got quiet again. I figured they must have passed out.

22

I came out on deck late the next morning. The sun was shining bright on the water, and after rubbing my eyes a bit, I lowered my hands only to see Cal, Frank, and Sam passed out on deck. Slate was walking up the dock. He came on board and said he was up all night and was going to get some sleep. Captain O'Keef was putting his dirty clothes in a bag while Nakee and me waited. He put the bag over his shoulder, and the three of us walked off to get breakfast.

Nakee and me had something called papaya juice with lime while Captain O'Keef had lots of coffee; then we were served up fish, eggs, toast, and a bowl of cut-up fruit. We finished eating and found a place to drop off the captain's clothes to get washed by a lady who had a business of washing people's clothes. As we walked through the city I noticed how different it was from the night before. I couldn't help but watch some cars on the roads. They honked their horns and made lots of noise. There were also carts pulled by horses and people walking all over the place. We went by a market with lots of food for sale. I expect that place would have been like heaven to Pa. There were goats, chickens, and pigs. There were lots of fruit and vegetables too. People were bartering and haggling with each other over what they wanted to buy or trade while others played music and sang in the distance.

We walked between the buildings, and I thought it must be something to live in one of them places. Then, Captain O'Keef pointed to the church. It was a beautiful place with two big towers, and I told him I'd be praying all day if I could go sit in that church. It wasn't like our chikee church back home; it was a civilized and proper church building that you could close up to keep the skeeters out.

Finally we reached the hotel where Captain O'Keef said we were to take a bath. Nakee and me followed the captain in and watched him give some money to a man behind the counter. We went upstairs, the captain unlocked the door, and we stepped into a big room with a big bed. Captain O'Keef showed me the bathtub and how to turn the water on. He told me that when the tub was full, to take my clothes off and sit in it. I had to scrub my whole body and hair with soap then rinse. The captain said, when I was done, Nakee was to do the same. He said he was going to get us the new clothes and he expected us to be bathed by the time he got back so we could go shopping for shoes.

I'd never been in a tub before, and it was lots of fun sloshing around in that thing making the water all bubbly. Nakee was in the other room and got tired of waiting his turn.

"Hurry up, Willie, it's my turn," he said, walking in from the other room. "Get out now!"

"No, you get out of here!" I yelled as I splashed water at him.

Across the room was a toilet bowl full of water; he reached in it and threw water at me. Then we started throwing water back and forth. The shiny tile floor was getting slippery with soap, so Nakee sat down and started pushing himself around the room with his hands; then he started pushing himself from one wall to the other. It looked like fun, so I got out of the tub and we were both slipping and sliding. We put more soap and water on the floor to make it more slippery and it was flowing into the other room, so we slid through the doorway and started playing in there too. We laid on our backs and put our feet on the walls to push off and slide faster. We even slid under the bed to the other side.

Nakee climbed on the bed and started jumping; then he yanked one of the sheets off, and we started pulling each other around the slippery floor with it. We were jumping on the bed, sliding on the floor, and laughing and yelling and having such a great time until someone started banging at the door. The man doing the banging was yelling real loud in Spanish so we didn't know what he was saying, but we could hear his keys jingle as he tried to open the door. Suddenly the door flung open, and when the man came in, he slipped on the wet floor and fell against the wall and onto the floor. First he looked surprised then; he got real mad and started yelling at us again. He was trying to get up but couldn't. By then other people were standing at the door looking in. I saw Captain O'Keef carrying packages and trying to make his way through all the people. He looked real mad, and we must have been quite a sight sitting on the floor all naked and wet with the bed such a mess. The captain threw the packages in and helped the man up; then that man started yelling at him. Captain O'Keef quickly pulled out some money and put a couple bills in the man's hand while carefully pushing him out and shutting the door behind him.

I picked up the wet sheet and started wiping the floor slowly as I watched Captain O'Keef look around the room. I could tell he was real disappointed in us. I looked around the room too and just couldn't believe how we got so carried away to make such a mess. There was soapy water everywhere.

"Willie did it," Nakee said quietly as he looked at Captain O'Keef then down at the floor.

I was ready to smack him sideways when he said that. "It wasn't just me!" I yelled at him.

He looked up at me and said sharply, "You started it, Willie!"

"Stop it!" Captain O'Keef shouted at us.

He carefully walked to the bed and pulled the other sheet off and threw it at Nakee. He said he already gave five dollars of our cow money to the man who slipped on the floor and if we didn't get that room cleaned up he was going to have to give him more to pay for this mess-up. Nakee and me started cleaning the room while Captain O'Keef went to take his bath. When he came out he laid on the bed and took a nap while Nakee and me, quietly, spent the rest of the morning cleaning.

When we were done we woke Captain O'Keef up, like he told us to. We opened the packages and put on the new clothes he bought for us. They were clean and crisp, and Nakee's shirt was too big, but Captain O'Keef said he'd grow into it soon enough. He put the bows around our necks, but we kept pulling them off until he finally gave up. Then, we put on the little caps. We didn't like the bows, but we liked the pants and shirt. The captain didn't get us shoes. He said we had to try them on to make sure they fit. When we were all ready we left the hotel and walked down the street all dressed up and barefoot until we reached a shoe store. The shoe man put stockings on our feet then showed us different kinds of shoes. We never had shoes on our feet before, and I could tell the man was getting annoyed because we wanted to try on all the shoes. We also had a hard time deciding between black or brown. Finally, we left the shoe store with shoes on our feet. It felt real uncomfortable to walk, but Captain O'Keef said we'd get use to them.

23

We decided to eat before heading back to the boat since it was already early afternoon and it would be a while before dinner. Captain O'Keef insisted we sit in a corner booth because he had something to tell us and we were supposed to be real quiet about it.

"I've got something for you boys," he said.

"What is it?" I asked.

"You have to promise you'll keep this real quiet and not tell anyone," he said.

"We promise, Captain O'Keef, we won't tell nobody," I said curiously.

"While I was out this morning I bought each of you a cowhide wallet," he said.

"What's that?" Nakee asked.

We looked at him real confused after he handed them to us. They were real nice and they had letters on them. Nakee opened his and put it on his head like a hat.

"Those are your initials," the captain explained.

We both stared at him, and Nakee took his wallet off his head and looked at the letters.

"Initials are the first letters of your first and last names. Nakee doesn't have a last name, so I made it the same as yours, Willie," he explained further.

We admired our new wallets with our initials on them, but we were not being real excited and looking real confused. The captain leaned over the table and continued to explain, in a soft voice, "They are used to hold money."

Then, he slid twenty dollars under each hand across the table for each of us to put inside our wallets. He put his finger over his lips and told us to keep quiet about it and stick the wallets in our pockets. He didn't want anyone knowing we had money. He said if anyone knew they'd be knocking us over the head to get it.

"This is part of your share of the money from the cows," he whispered; then he said softly, "Keep it in your wallets real safe and don't show or tell anyone."

I don't need to say how Nakee and me could hardly contain ourselves over our brand-new cowhide wallets with real hard-earned money inside. We both felt proud of ourselves, and we knew right then that we found a home with Captain O'Keef. We knew that he was the best man anyone could ever know and we were so lucky to have him in our lives, taking care of us.

After lunch, Captain O'Keef made Nakee and me go back to the boat to practice reading. He said he was going to take care of some things, which included picking up his clothes from the wash lady. He said he'd see us back at the boat.

Nakee and me were walking down the street when I saw his hand holding his pocket open. He was looking down at his new wallet. Then he reached in and started lifting it out.

"Nakee, you best put that thing back in your pocket before I take it from you," I ordered firmly but quietly.

"Why? Why can't I just hold it?" he asked.

"You can hold it when we get back to the boat. If you don't put it back, I'll tell Captain O'Keef," I threatened.

When we boarded the *Bonnie Sue* nobody was there, so we immediately went below and took out our wallets. We admired our new wallets for a long time and studied the money carefully, reading each letter and number on it.

"Whatcha gonna do with your money, Willie?" Nakee asked.

"Don't know yet. What about you?" I asked back.

"Well, being as I can't take it outta my pocket in front uh people, how's I supposed to spend it?" he snapped back at me.

He was still mad because I threatened to tell on him.

"I just wanted you to be careful and not be so foolish, 'specially after what we did this morning at the hotel. I don't ever want Captain O'Keef disappointed in us ever again," I told him.

He looked at me and looked back down at his wallet. "Yeah, you're right," he said.

Just then we heard Cal, Frank, and Sam come on board. We quick put our money in our wallets and back in our pockets. We pulled a book out and together started looking for words we knew.

"Look below, look and see who's here," we heard Cal order.

Sam looked down at us and smiled.

"It's just them birdbrain kids looking at a book," Sam yelled as he turned and walked away.

"We ain't birdbrains, Sam!" Nakee yelled.

"Sam's just jealous 'cause he can't read," I called out real loud.

It was getting late and Captain O'Keef wasn't back yet. It would be dark soon, and I figured it wouldn't be long before those three men would start drinking. I also wondered where Slate had gone off to. The last we saw of him was in the morning when after being out all night, he came on board and said he was going to sleep.

I told Nakee it would be best if we went to look for Captain O'Keef and Slate. Havana was bigger than any place I'd been to and there were lots of people, so I decided the best place to start was at the wash lady's place. We were walking toward her house, and I noticed a lot of people gathered down the street a few blocks over. There wasn't any music, and a lot of people were yelling at each other in Spanish. We started walking toward them, but just then someone grabbed us both by the arm and pulled us away.

"Slate!" I yelled, looking up at him.

"No, no, no. You boys need to come with me!" he said.

"We's come to look for you 'n the captain," Nakee said to him.

"Do you know where Captain O'Keef is?" I asked while trying to push his hand off my arm.

He was pulling us along with him, and his grip was holding us real tight.

"What are you doing?" I yelled. "Let me go!"

I asked him to tell me why he was taking us away from all those people, and just then Nakee managed to squirm out of his new shirt, leaving it hanging in Slate's grip.

"What's going on over there that you don't want us to see?" he yelled at Slate.

Slate turned to grab him, but Nakee was running down the street toward the crowd. Slate let go of me and ran after Nakee. He turned back at me and, with his finger pointed right at me, ordered for me to stay there. I knew he was serious, so I stood there watching him as he ran to get Nakee, but as soon as I saw Nakee get lost in the crowd in front of Slate, I started running toward them.

I pushed my way through the crowd then heard a real loud scream over and over and it wouldn't stop. I was pushing and ducking to get through the people; then I looked up and saw it was Nakee screaming so loud. He was punching, screaming, and crying as Slate carried him away, and I didn't understand what was going on. I started yelling at Slate to put him down then found myself in the middle of the crowd. That's when I saw him—Captain O'Keef! He was laying on the ground.

"Captain O'Keef! What happened?" I yelled, realizing something was awful wrong.

Blood, there was blood everywhere, and all the people's voices suddenly blurred together. I kept calling his name, but he just laid there with his eyes open. I started sobbing uncontrollably. I felt sick. It was like my stomach suddenly turned inside out, and I started spewing all over the place. People were backing away because it was splattering on their shoes. I looked at them and asked for help. I picked up Captain O'Keef's hand and tried to pull him up. He was heavy and he wouldn't get up, so I got down and just held on to him and hugged him. I could tell he was gone and I didn't know what to do. I couldn't bear the loss of such a kind man who I grew to love so much. He was my friend, my teacher; he was the pa any boy would long for. How could Nakee and me go on without him? I kept hugging him with my head on his chest. His shirt was wet with all my tears. I was covered in his blood and my own spew, and I just sobbed.

Slate handed Nakee to a big woman standing outside of the crowd then came back for me. I didn't want to go; I couldn't go. A man helped Slate peel me off the captain's chest as I tried to hang on. I started hitting but didn't have the strength to fight. I went limp as Slate carried me over to the big lady holding Nakee tight in her arms while he cried. When I saw him, Slate put me down and I went to him and hugged him real tight and we cried together. Slate told us there was nothing we could do. The officials were going to take care of things and we'd see them in the morning. He grabbed Nakee's shirt from the lady and threw it over his shoulder; then he grabbed our hands and started leading us away slowly.

24

Back at the boat, Slate made us a drink with pineapple juice and rum, hoping it would help us sleep; then he washed my shirt so it would be dry by morning. Nakee and I cried most of the night, but eventually we did get some sleep. It was late that morning when Slate woke us up. He was back from seeing the officials and making arrangements with the undertaker.

I was already missing Captain O'Keef, and there was an empty, sick feeling inside me that I thought would never go away. I didn't know how to cope with so much pain in my heart. I looked over at Nakee and saw him laying in his hammock just staring at the ceiling. His eyes were red and teary and he was whimpering softly. We were wore out, and I didn't think we would ever be able to smile or laugh again. I knew I had to be there for Nakee. He was all I had, and I had to make him strong again. We both had to be strong to survive, and we needed each other more than ever.

I could tell that Slate was sad when he came over to talk to me.

"I've made the funeral arrangements for this afternoon," he said.

I could feel the tears suddenly rolling down my face again as I laid there in my hammock. I stared at the captain's books on the shelf. I wanted to know all that was inside them books.

"Willie!" Slate said softly. "Are you hearing me? You need to get up. We have to get ready."

Slate was gently rubbing my shoulder while trying to convince me that we needed to go. I knew that he too was grieving over the loss of his good friend the captain, and I was just making it harder for him, so I gathered what strength I had and got up. Slate brought my clean shirt to me and I got dressed.

After Nakee and me were ready we walked to the big church to pray. Cal, Frank, and Sam had already gone the church, and the thought of them being there made me angry inside. I knew they didn't really care about Captain O'Keef. I didn't think Cal, like Pa, cared about anybody but himself.

As we went into the church, I heard the choir singing and I saw angels on the walls. It was beautiful. That church must have been the closest place to God in the whole world, and I felt somewhat comforted by that. If I had to choose a place to pray for Captain O'Keef, that was it.

People sat on benches and others kneeled. The priest prayed at the altar, and two boys were lighting candles. Me, Slate, and Nakee sat on a bench close to the front and listened to the choir for a while; then we prayed. The priest spoke for a while, but none of us could understand what he was saying. I didn't know much about praying, and it was too painful to think about what we were here for. First, I thought about how much the captain meant to me and how I would miss him. Then, I had to think about Nakee and what to hope for in my life without Captain O'Keef. I just tried to think about that.

We left the church and walked up the road a ways to the cemetery. Three men leaning on their shovels were on a hill near a tree waiting for us. As we got closer I could see a big wooden box. It didn't seem real that in that box was Captain O'Keef. It didn't seem real that just yesterday we were having lunch and talking with him. He gave us our new wallets. I reached into my pocket to see if maybe I was dreaming about all this, but there it was, my new wallet in my new pants, and there we were standing in the graveyard with our new shoes on, getting ready to lay the captain to rest forever.

We stayed until the burial was over and the cement cross with his name on it was placed on the grave. We walked to the market and got flowers then went back to lay them on his grave and say goodbye

for the last time. I was glad Cal, Sam, and Frank left and didn't come with us to get the flowers.

I turned my attention to Nakee. We were on our own now, and I had to think of what to do. Slate took us to eat, and we sat at a table outside where a lady brought us our food. I had not thought about what happened to Captain O'Keef or even why he was killed until Nakee brought it up.

"Did someone knock him over the head and kill him to take his money?" Nakee asked as he started to cry.

"Maybe," Slate said. "I do know that he didn't have money on him when I got there and the officials are investigating. Hopefully they'll find the captain's killer."

"If I find him I'll kill him! I swear I'll kill him!" I yelled. I banged my fist on the table as I jumped up and turned around crying; then I ran as fast as I could toward the boat.

I had never been so angry ever in my life. I was sweating from running so fast, and when I saw the *Bonnie Sue* in front of me, my

body went limp and I collapsed on the dock. Nakee had been running after me, and Slate had rushed to pay and have the lady wrap our food up for us. When he reached us, we were both sitting on the dock crying. He made us get on the boat, gave us the bag of food, and told us to stay there and eat.

"We're leaving in the morning," Slate said; then he turned and walked away.

All I could think of was that we were going to leave Captain O'Keef behind laying in a box in the ground next to a tree. He wasn't going back with us, and we'd never see him again. It was early evening, and Nakee and me were too tired to eat. We spent the rest of the evening crying ourselves to sleep.

25

We were already underway when I woke up the next morning. I was real hungry, so after laying in my hammock for a while, I decided to get up. I put my leg over the side and stepped onto the corner of a crate. I looked down and saw crates all over the floor. There was hardly a place on the floor to step. I was curious, so I got down and saw the letters on the crates, R-U-M, it said.

"Rrruuumm," I said, trying to read it. "Ruumm, rum!" Then I yelled real loud, "It's rum! We's taking back rum! Captain O'Keef said he didn't want no rum on his boat!"

I yelled for Slate, and Nakee woke up.

"Why are you yelling?" Nakee asked.

"Slate!" I yelled, demanding an explanation. "Why's there rum on Captain O'Keef's boat?"

Nakee looked down from his hammock and saw all the crates. "Is that rum in them crates?" he asked.

I grabbed my hatchet and started hacking at one of the crates. I was so angry at that moment. I pried a board up and grabbed two bottles of rum; then I stomped out on deck, flinged the two bottles overboard, and demanded again an explanation.

Just then Cal ran over and grabbed my wrist real tight. I was ready to punch him, but he yanked me toward him, grabbing my other hand. He said, "You best not touch one more of them bottles or I'll be throwing you overboard myself!"

He dragged me to the rail and pushed my head over the side; then he picked up one of my legs high in the air and threatened, "You wanna be eaten by sharks like them cows? You best do as you're told, boy."

I was so scared he was going to drop me into the ocean, but right then he pulled back and threw me down on the deck. Nakee ran over and knelt down next to me. I could tell he was scared because he didn't say anything. We both watched Cal and waited to see what he was going to do next, but he just turned and walked away.

Cal glared at Slate then pointed at me and threatened, "He best not pull another stunt like that again or we'll be dumpin' the three of ya over."

Slate came over to help me up. We knew he meant it, so we walked away quietly. Slate explained how he tried to keep them from loading the rum but couldn't. He said he was getting off when we reached Key West because if we got caught he didn't want to go to jail. He explained that Nakee and me were too young to go to jail and we had to go back to Millie's and stay as far away from Cal, Sam, and Frank as possible.

The weather wasn't looking too good that morning, and later the seas started getting rough. I was below with Nakee, thinking about what to do. I thought about the *Bonnie Sue* and realized those men were going to keep her for themselves. If that were true, I was going to take Captain O'Keef's things. The wind was picking up and the waves were getting bigger, so I knew the men would be busy on deck. The boat was rocking hard, but I managed to pick the lock to the captain's quarters; then Nakee and me went in to look around. The captain had all his navigation charts and some books on a shelf. All his clothes were stowed in a locker except the ones he took to the wash lady in Cuba. We held on tight as we looked through the lockers. First, we found a small compass and a knife. Then we found his gun. It was the gun he used to shoot the cows and the pirates. We put all those things in a canvas bag; then we found a box with important papers and under it was a hole in the floor. There was a small leather bag with money in it! It must have been some of the cow money. I put the leather bag with the money in the canvas bag with the gun, the compass, and the knife; then I put books in it too. Nakee found a framed picture of Captain O'Keef hanging in a locker. He was on the bed staring at it all teary-eyed, and to tell you the truth, when I saw it, I got a lump in my throat and could hardly hold back the tears, but I knew we needed to get out of there. I grabbed the picture and put it in the bag; then I told Nakee to get out so I could lock the door.

I put the canvas bag next to my hammock in the locker with my hatchet, and we both climbed into our hammocks where we stayed for the rest of the day. We didn't want to even look at those evil men. I was scared of them and worried about what they might do to us if they found out we were in the captain's quarters. Slate came down a few times, after the weather cleared up, to talk to us and make sure we were all right. He also fixed us something to eat.

It was almost dark when we set anchor just east of Key West behind a mangrove island. Nakee and me stayed in our hammocks until morning when Slate was packing up to leave. I asked him if we could go with him, and he said he thought it best if we went to the mainland. He told us to go to Millie's because she could get us food and help us find a safe place to stay.

We watched Slate get into the dory and leave with Cal and Frank. They rowed him ashore, and I was only hoping I'd see him again someday. Sam told us to peel potatoes so we could fix dinner. He said Cal and Frank had business to take care of in Key West and he'd be ashore for a while. I was afraid for Slate. I found out what kind of business Cal and Frank were up to because they returned the next morning on another boat with two men. They brought back the dory and hoisted it on board; then Sam, Frank, and one of the other men transferred crates of rum onto the other boat, and as I watched from the companionway, I saw a man give Cal a lot of money. He had sold some of the rum.

Cal told Frank to go below and see how many crates were left and said not to forget to count the ones in the fish hold; then they each counted their share of the rum money. I was glad to know that Nakee and me would be away from them soon. We weighed anchor and were on our way again, and I thought we'd be sailing into the night because we left so late, but after crossing the Florida Bay we set anchor off Cape Sable for the night.

I was still hurting from what happened to the captain, and I wasn't sleeping too well. During the night I was easily awakened by men's whispering voices, and it was coming from the captain's quarters.

I wondered what they were doing in Captain O'Keef's quarters, so I got down to look. The rum crates under my hammock were gone, so I quietly stepped on the floor and sneaked over to the door-way. I noticed the key in the keyhole of the captain's door. How'd they get that key? Captain O'Keef always had it with him on a chain around his neck. I looked into the room carefully so they wouldn't see me. The lantern next to the captain's bed was lit.

"The rest'a that money's gotta be here somewhere," I heard Cal whisper sharply.

"Ya shoulda made him tell us first; how's we gonna find it now?" the other man whispered back. I thought it was Frank, but I could tell, Sam was in there too.

"Shut up! I'll tear this boat up if I have to. It's gotta be here somewhere," Cal whispered.

They were looking for the money I found earlier in the captain's leather bag. They were going to steal it! I was real puzzled by what was going on but didn't want them to see me, so I quietly went back to my hammock. I laid there thinking about the captain, his key, and the money; then I fell asleep for a while until the sun came up and we were already heading out. After sailing all day we heard the men lowering some sails, so Nakee and me went on deck. We were happy to see the docks near Millie's place, and we couldn't wait to tie up and get off that boat.

As we got closer to the dock I followed Nakee below to get our things. I found another bag for Nakee and told him to put some books in it with his things. There were sixteen books, and I wanted to take them with us. The books were heavy, but I didn't care; they were the captain's books and I wanted them. I tied my hatchet around my waist and we went back up on deck. Cal saw us with the bags and walked over to us.

"Whatcha got in them bags?" he asked, grabbing the bag out of my hand. "You stealin' stuff off the boat?" he continued, questioning me suspiciously.

"Books! We're taking the captain's books!" I snapped back at him. I grabbed hold of the bag and tried to pull it away from him. I was scared he'd find out what was in it.

Frank and Sam started laughing. "Let 'em have them stupid books," Frank said. "We ain't got no use for 'em."

"Willie's gonna read me them stories every night like Captain O'Keef did," Nakee said sadly.

I was sure glad when Nakee said that because it convinced Cal that I was telling the truth, and he agreed to give them to us. He pushed the bag hard into my chest. He leaned over, looked me in the eyes, and said that if we squealed about the rum he'd come after us and hurt us real bad and maybe kill us. Then he turned and lit a cigarette. Without any more questions he let us walk off the boat carrying our bags. I wasn't about to tell anyone about the rum because I believed Cal when he said he'd come after us and I wanted him as far away from us as possible.

The books were heavy, and we struggled to carry our bags over to Millie's. We told her what happened on our trip. I could tell Millie was real sad about the captain; she had known him a long time.

Later she turned her attention to us and asked what we were going to do. She was concerned and without giving me a chance to answer, she quickly said she was going to find us a home with some real nice people in town. Millie lived in a house behind the dining place, so she told us to go there and get cleaned up; she'd be there in the evening after she closed Millie's.

26

Nakee and I got cleaned up at Millie's, and we waited in her front room. I was sitting there thinking about the men in the captain's quarters during the night. What were they doing and how did they get the key? Then in my mind I remembered seeing the key in the door and I remembered the chain was hanging from it. How'd they get the chain? Why did they say, "The rest'a that money" and "Ya shoulda made him tell us first"? How did they know he wasn't carrying all the money?

"They stole the captain's money and they was looking for more; they's the killers!" I whispered slowly as I thought about it.

I ran over to Nakee, knelt down next to where he was sitting, and said real fast in a whispery voice, "They's the killers, Nakee! They's the killers! They killed Captain O'Keef!"

"What? Who? Who killed Captain O'Keef?" Nakee whispered back.

"Cal, Cal killed him! Cal and Sam and Frank killed the captain! They killed him," I whispered back then quickly explained. "They killed him then they took his key from around his neck and they took his money but he left part of it on the boat. It's the money we found in the leather bag; I saw them looking for it last night."

Nakee looked at me real confused and said, "How do you know that? Why would they kill him?"

"Money, that cow money wasn't good enough for them and that's why they wanted rum so they could sell it and get more money," I said, suddenly realizing that I had to stay calm.

If they got wind that we knew what they'd done, they'd kill us for sure.

"But Captain O'Keef was a nice man. He was nice to everybody," Nakee said.

"Them men ain't nice! They's mean, evil men and they's going to pay for what they done to Captain O'Keef," I snapped back.

"We's going to tell the officials what they done?" Nakee asked.

"No," I said. "There's no way of getting back to Cuba. They took the captain's money and they's gonna take his boat too but I won't let 'em have it. They's got some of his money but I won't let 'em have the *Bonnie Sue*. Never!"

"What's we gonna do, Willie? How's we gonna take the *Bonnie Sue* away from them men?" Nakee asked.

"We's not!" I answered. Then I explained, "We's gonna burn it! We's going to set fire to the *Bonnie Sue* tonight and burn her up and you best not tell a soul 'bout this or we'll be in jail or killed."

I emptied our bags and put all the books in one bag with our shoes. Then, I put what we needed in the other bag with the captain's things. We could carry that bag with us and leave the bag with the books and shoes at Millie's. We were going to be on the run after burning that boat, and I didn't need books or shoes slowing us down.

Millie brought us lunch and made sure we had everything we needed. Then, all afternoon Nakee and me planned how we could set the *Bonnie Sue* on fire. I was real good at starting fires, but I had to be fast and not get caught. I looked around Millie's kitchen and found matches; then we waited until after Millie got off work because we didn't want her out looking for us.

After we all settled in to sleep for the night, I got up and tied my hatchet around my waist then grabbed the bag. Nakee and I sneaked out. We went around the train station where most of the lights were out. There was a tavern nearby, and we heard people laughing and talking real loud. I heard Sam's voice. He was calling for Cal to get another bottle of rum. They were out drinking, and that was good for us.

We sneaked down to the docks, and I told Nakee to stay behind the bushes till I got back. I said I'd be back real quick after I got the fire started. I was going to leave the bag with him, but it worried me some because he wasn't real good at doing what he was told, so instead I tied the bag to my back. I told him they'd kill me if I got caught so I'd have to leave him behind if he wasn't there when I got back.

He promised me he'd stay there, so I started working my way down toward the *Bonnie Sue*. I walked under the dock until I reached the water; then I climbed up on the dock and bent down and started running. Everything was real still. I jumped on the *Bonnie Sue* and went into the cabin. The crates of rum were still on board. I was glad because it meant they were going to burn too.

None of the lanterns were lit, but I knew my way around the cabin well and found the crate I had opened with my hatchet. I pushed it between two other crates in the middle of the cabin and turned it on its side; then I pulled the straw out for kindling. Oil would make the fire spread fast, so I collected all the lanterns. I took the lids off and tossed lots of oil forward; then I poured some on the open crate so it would drip down slowly and eventually onto the straw. Finally, I lit the straw with a match and quickly poured as much oil as I could around the companionway before I stepped out. I jumped off the boat and lifted the stern line real fast over the piling and pushed the stern away from the dock. Then, I ran as fast as I could down the dock, jumped off to the side onto the sandy beach, and kept running up into the bushes where Nakee was still waiting.

"Where's the fire?" Nakee asked.

I turned around quickly and saw there was no fire.

"Oh, no!" I said. "It musta gone out!"

We sat there behind the bush staring at the *Bonnie Sue*. I was real disappointed that my fire went out and was thinking of what to do next, when suddenly with a roar, a light flashed and it started burning. The oil must have finally dripped onto the fire. It was perfect.

The fire started burning real fierce; then all the rum bottles started exploding with the heat. It was some sight. Lights everywhere were coming on, and people were yelling and running to the docks. Fishermen were trying to get their boats untied and away from the fire. We saw Cal, Sam, and Frank running to the boat, and right then I knew we needed to get out of there.

We ran into the woods when suddenly I stopped and realized that it would be better if we could sneak back into Millie's house. Nakee had been running behind me, and I told him we had to get back to Millie's so she would think we were there all night and nobody would know we did this. We had to go to Millie's. When we got to her house, we hid next to the front porch, when suddenly her lights came on. All the noise outside must have woken her, and she ran out the door and down her front porch to see what was happening. That's when we ran up behind her.

"What's happening, Millie?" I yelled real loud.

She turned around and said she didn't know. She told us to go inside and she was going to find out. We ran in, and I put the bag under the bed and the matches back in the kitchen. Then Nakee and me ran outside. We caught up with Millie near the docks, and by then someone had managed to cut the bowline and push the *Bonnie Sue* away from the dock. It was still burning, and I was glad but real sad to see her go like that. It was right then that I learned, like chapters in books we have chapters in our lives and this ended one for me.

27

We were eating breakfast at Millie's place and could see the *Bonnie Sue* half-sunk in the back bay. Everyone was talking about what or who could have started the fire. Suddenly Cal, Sam, and Frank came in with some men following behind them. A man was yelling at Cal, and we could tell he was mad.

"We paid for the goods and you didn't deliver so we want our money back!" he yelled; then he grabbed the back of Cal's shirt and pulled him sideways.

Cal slapped his hand away and said, "I told you to get them crates off the boat and you didn't, so how's that my fault?" Then Cal pushed him away.

"And I told you we couldn't get 'em till morning," that man answered back, gritting his teeth.

It turns out that Cal sold him the crates of rum that burned. Cal wouldn't give him his money back and the rum was gone, so that man wasn't real happy. Suddenly he punched Cal right in the face and knocked him down. Sam and Frank jumped on that man, and the other men jumped on Sam and Frank, and they all started fighting; then everyone else started yelling and fighting and things were flying all over the place. One of those men was yelling that he was going to kill Cal. Nakee and me got scared and threw ourselves on the floor next to the wall, crawled quickly to the door, and ran into Millie's house. I told Nakee to never tell a soul because any one of those men would kill us over what we'd done. Millie saw us leave and came after us. We told her we didn't want to stay there anymore.

"Where ya gonna go?" she asked, sounding real concerned.

"I know my kinfolk come from a place inland so we's gonna go find 'em," I lied. Then I said, "We can't carry the captain's books, so we want you to keep 'em for us if you would, please. We hopes to be back for 'em one day,"

Millie was nice enough and agreed to keep the books for us, but I wasn't really sure we'd ever be back and I was sorry to leave them. I wanted Nakee and me to each pick one book to take with us, so I chose *Moby Dick*. Nakee didn't know which one to get, so I chose *Treasure Island* for him. I couldn't read too well, but I figured someday if I practiced enough I'd be able to read every word like Captain O'Keef. We put the two books in the bag and said goodbye to Millie. I was grateful when she gave us two loafs of bread to take with us. We'd be needing that, so I thanked her and she hugged us both and told us to be careful then we headed out.

We followed close to the shoreline and saw a fisherman getting ready to go out on his skiff. He was going to cross the harbor to his homestead where he lived with his wife and kids, and we were lucky enough to get a ride from that man. When we got across, he asked us if we wanted to go to his house, but we told him we had to be on our way. I asked him if there was a trail going east. He told us to walk until we saw the automobile trail then head south on it and when we got to the river we could follow it east. So we started walking.

"Where's we gonna go, Willie?" Nakee asked as we headed down the trail.

"I don't know, Nakee. All I knows is we can't stay where we was and we can't go west so I figured we'd just head east. I've never been east before and I reckon it's probably as good a way to go as any."

We didn't say much else. We walked a while then stopped and ate some of Millie's bread. It filled our bellies enough to get us going again, and we walked the rest of the day. It was going to be dark soon, and it was a comfortably cool evening. We hiked into the scrub a ways and set up camp on a sandy clearing then started a fire to keep us warm, also, to keep the skeeters and animals away. We were tired, so we fell asleep real quick and slept sound through the night.

I woke up to a strange noise, and it was getting louder as it got closer.

"Nakee! Wake up! Wake up! Hurry," I said as I leaned over to shake him awake.

I jumped up and kicked sand on the fire then grabbed the bag and my hatchet and yelled back at Nakee to get up. I ran through the scrub to the edge of the automobile trail and watched from behind a scrub palm. As Nakee caught up with me, we saw it. It was an automobile coming down the trail. As it got closer we saw a man and a woman in it and they were dressed real fancy, so I thought they might be nice enough to give us a ride. I walked out on the trail and waved my arms, and when they got close they stopped. The man looked old. It looked like he had no hair under his hat, and he had a real big belly. He was smoking a big cigar, and the lady was young and kind of pretty when she smiled at me. They were riding in a nice big black car, and they looked real comfortable in that car.

"What are you doing out here in the middle of nowhere?" the man yelled over to me.

"I'm going home to my kinfolk," I lied. "I'll be heading inland once I reach the river." I looked down at my feet. "Sir, I'm real tired. Would you be kind enough to give us a ride to the river?" I asked as Nakee walked out onto the road behind me.

"Us?" he said, trying to see behind me. "Who's that?" he asked when he saw Nakee.

"It's Nakee. He's traveling with me," I said.

"But he's one of them native boys," said the man. "I ain't havin' no native boy riding in my car. You can come, but not him!" he said in a loud and gruff voice.

"Aw, can't we give the boys a ride?" the lady said. "Do something kind for these poor boys." She smiled at him. "Please?"

She was persuasive enough to convince him to take us both. The man smiled back at her real nice then turned and frowned at

us. He got out and clumsily put the canvas top on the car down. He opened the door for us, and we were happy to hop into the back seat. I suppose he wanted to get fresh air on account of not liking the smell of us being in his nice car.

I told the man that Nakee and me never rode in an automobile before and how we appreciated him letting us ride with him. I asked him if it was a long way to the river, and he said it wasn't too far by car. Nakee and me sat back and enjoyed the ride.

When we reached the river he turned and drove east for a while until we reached a wooden bridge. The man stopped the car for us to get out and told us to follow the road to the lake and go north and around it. We thanked them and said goodbye. The nice lady smiled and waved back at us as they headed toward the bridge.

28

We started walking east along the road, and Nakee was walking behind me not saying much when he pulled my shirt real hard. I turned to look at him when he put his finger over his mouth and pointed through the scrub to a deer far in the distance. I ducked down, pulling him with me. It was too far to throw my hatchet at him, so I thought about what to do; then I slowly stuck my hand in the bag and felt around for the gun while I watched the deer. I didn't know anything about guns, but I saw Captain O'Keef use it a couple of times, so I thought it would be real easy to shoot a deer just like he shot the cows. Nakee reached up quietly and covered his ears as I took the gun out and pointed it right at that deer's chest. I was preparing myself for a loud "Bang!" but when I pulled the trigger it just snapped. The deer jumped and ran away. There was no loud "Bang!" and I didn't understand what happened, so I put the gun back in the bag, tied it to my back, and we kept walking. I was confused and disappointed at not getting that deer, but at that time I didn't know about bullets. We walked a long way, hoping to see another deer. We talked about how to kill one and cook it up for dinner; then we started hearing lots of noise and men talking loud and in the distance. We saw piles of dirt along the shore and two barges in the river. We sneaked up close to watch men with horses working to clear the shoreline. Some of the men had chains on their legs.

"What's them men doin' and why's they in chains?" Nakee asked.

I didn't know so I shrugged and told him to be quiet.

"Look!" Nakee said. "Over there. Look at that man."

I looked over at a group of men working. Those men didn't have chains on, but there were men with rifles and whips watching over them, guarding them and making them work. Suddenly, I saw a young man who looked familiar. Nakee was pointing at him.

"That's Micco, one of them older village boys! What's he doin' here?" Nakee asked.

"Who?" I asked. Then I remembered. "Micco, that's the rope lady's son! The lady in the village who gave us the rope for my hatchet, that's her son! Why's he here?" I asked, not understanding the situation.

I knew something was really wrong because when he turned, I saw scars and a long cut on his back. I could tell he was having a hard time working. That cut must have been hurting him real bad. Why was Micco there? Why were they making him work so hard? I couldn't answer that, but I was going to find out. We couldn't leave the rope lady's son there after she was so nice to us.

We watched Micco while I was thinking of what to do. He looked real tired and stopped working. One of the guards walked to him, whipped him, and told him to get back to work. After that, I knew I had to do something but had to wait for the right time.

A car drove up, and a well-dressed man got out and walked around. He started talking to a guard and pointed at Micco and two other men. We heard him tell the guard that he couldn't afford to lose anyone and to give those workers water and let them rest in the shade. The guard with the whip went to get Micco and the two men; then he made two men in chains join them. He slowly guided them to an area behind the big piles of dirt and made them sit under a tree. Nakee and me sneaked around through the scrub to where we could see Micco. Another guard brought them water then left. I told Nakee that this would be our only chance to save Micco so we needed to do something fast.

I thought about how I sneaked up to that gator and hit him with my hatchet, but I hadn't practiced throwing it for a long time. The guard with the rifle circled around Micco and the other men, and every once in a while he stopped to poke one with his rifle. Maybe he was seeing if they looked good enough to go back to work.

I watched him go around and I knew he'd be coming close to me again, so I turned and signaled for Nakee to go. I whispered that he needed to leave to get a head start and we'd catch up. When he left, I got ready with my hatchet and waited until he stopped. I lifted and aimed the hatchet at his foot. Then I threw it harder than I'd ever thrown it.

Suddenly, the guard screamed as he fell to the ground, dropping his rifle. He reached down and quick pulled my hatchet out of his foot, threw it aside, and grabbed his foot. He sat on the ground screaming in agony while the men sitting with Micco stood up quickly and started running as fast as they could. One man grabbed the rifle and shot the man and the screaming stopped. I ran to get my hatchet and I quickly saw that it had hacked through the dead guard's shoe to the bone and he was bleeding all over the place. I waved for Micco to come, and we started running through the scrub. The guards at the river were coming around the dirt pile shooting, and as we ran we could see the men on the other side had started running in all directions. The confusion had the guards running and shooting all over the place. Micco was weak, so I grabbed his hand and pulled him along behind me, and we ran fast as we could for our lives. Nakee saw us through the scrub and started running after us, and we ran as far as we could before we had to rest.

We slowed down to catch our breath and fell to the ground real tired. I sat there staring at Micco when suddenly he said, "Thank you" to me.

Micco explained to Nakee that he had been there for a long time and learned how to speak a little English. Nakee told me that Micco said he was out hunting far from the village when some white men saw him and chased him through the scrub. They caught him and took him to that place to work. He said there were prisoners from many jails working there.

"Called work gang," Micco said. "I not prisoner so no chain but still make me work hard."

"What's that they're doing with all that dirt?" I asked.

"They build waterway to big lake," he answered.

"Why?" I asked.

"For boats," he answered.

I didn't understand but knew we had to be on our way, so we started walking with the sun at our backs, and before long it was time to set up camp again. We were out of bread and real hungry, so while I started the fire Micco and Nakee went to look for something to eat. I cut the heart out of a small scrub palm, and they brought back a gopher turtle. We butchered it up and cooked it over the fire. We had a real good meal that night; then we went to sleep.

The next morning we woke up early and started following the road, paying attention in case we were to see an automobile in the distance coming toward us so we could run into the scrub and not be seen. We were heading east with the sun in our eyes that morning when Micco asked why we left the village. We spent the day as we walked telling the story of what had happened to us. We asked him about Tayki, and he said that she cried a lot when we didn't come back. He told us how she was sad for a long time and always believed we would come back to her someday. Right then, Nakee and me decided that since we didn't have anywhere to go that we should go back to the village with Micco. He said we wouldn't be able to get through the swamp if we went south, so we had to go north around the big lake then go east before we could head south to find our way to the village.

Micco never asked us why we saved him, but we knew he was grateful to us. I thought of how life changes a person's way of thinking and even though Nakee and me was nonhuman boys we were still good. We thought Micco was good too, and we knew we could be friends because were getting along real well as we traveled east. It was better traveling with Micco because he knew how to get food. He was good at catching snakes, and he also cooked up weevil grubs like those Pa ate back at the shack and they weren't all that bad.

We walked and camped next to the roads for many days. We reached the big lake and headed north following a dirt trail. When we saw or heard cars or trucks in the distance, we quickly hid in the scrub until they passed; then we waited until they were a long way ahead of us. Micco said that if they caught us they would snatch us up, take away our freedom, and make us work.

Nakee saw something in the distance behind us.

"Someone's coming! Hide!" he yelled.

We ran into the scrub and waited, but we couldn't hear it and it was taking a long time to pass us.

"That automobile should have passed us by now," I said to my friends.

"Where is it?" Nakee asked, sounding very concerned.

"Shhhh. I'm going to go out to the road to see where it is, so you get ready to run if I yell. I'll catch up with you," I told them.

I creeped out to the road and I saw it, but it was still a long way behind us. I thought maybe the car or truck was broken. Maybe they were pushing it. I went back into the scrub and told Micco and Nakee what I saw, and we all decided we would sit and wait until it passed.

We waited a long time. Then we heard people talking but there was no automobile noise.

"It's them," Micco whispered. "Let's get outta here."

I told him to wait. I wanted to go look again. Nakee and Micco were very impatient and wanted to go deeper into the scrub, but I told them I was going to see who these people who took so long to reach us were. I stayed low and hid behind the scrub palms until I reached the road. I stuck my head out beyond a palm frond just enough so I could see who was coming down the road. It was a mule pulling a wagon. No wonder it took so long to reach us. Sitting in the front driving the mule was a very old black man, and sitting next to him was an old black lady. They carried a bunch of stuff in the wagon, and as they passed me I saw a boy, a little black boy almost as big as Nakee sitting in the back. They were heading up the road getting farther and farther away, and I didn't want to miss my chance of getting a ride from these folks because I was sure tired of walking. I looked up and down that dirt road and didn't see anybody else, so

I decided right then I was going to meet these folks and maybe, just maybe, they'd be nice enough to give us a ride, so I started running after them.

"Hey! Stop! Hey, sir, stop!" I yelled.

I was waving my cap in the air and running real fast to catch up. The little boy just sat there staring at me. The old lady must have heard me because she turned around, reached over, and shook the man's shoulder and pointed at me. The man pulled on the reins to stop and turned around as I was catching up to them.

He looked at me and said, "Boy whatcha doin out here in da middle o' noplace?"

I had stopped and was bent over catching my breath; then I stood up straight as I explained to the man how we needed a ride. The little boy had gotten up and was standing on the wagon, real close, behind the old lady riding on the front bench next to the old man.

"We? Who we? I just sees you. Who you got witchu?" the old man asked as he jerked his head up and looked around with his eyes open real wide.

"There's three of us, sir. Won't ya please give us a ride? We's real tired of walkin' and we'll be good at catchin' food for y'all," I pleaded.

I called out for Nakee and Micco to come out and meet the folks. And before long we were in the wagon headed east. We sat in the back with the little boy, but he didn't say much.

"What's ya name?" I asked, but he just stared at me with a curious look on his face.

"I said, what's ya name? Can't you hear?" I asked.

He looked at me and just nodded.

"Then, what's ya name?" I asked again.

"Maybe he can't talk," Nakee said.

"He scared. Black people scared of whites, people in village scared of whites too," Micco said.

Suddenly the little boy said. "Bo, my name Bo."

We all looked at him kind of surprised; then I thought of what Captain O'Keef would have done.

"Hi, Bo," I said, "it's good to meet ya," and after that, I introduced us to Bo. "I's Willie and this is my brother Nakee and our friend Micco."

We continued down the road slowly until late in the day; then we pulled off into a little area of scrub to set up camp. I was eager to find good food for them folks like I said we would, so after we got the fire going we went looking for dinner. We were on the edge of the marshland, so Micco was going to see if he could get us a gator. He was much bigger than me and had experience hunting gators, so he went to get one while Nakee and me followed. I gave him my hatchet to use, and sure enough he was able to get a small gator. It was just big enough for us to enjoy a good meal that night, and our new black friends were mighty thankful to us.

After dinner we sat around the fire and talked and got to know each other some, and they were real nice folks. They told us their son Aysen was Bo's pa. He got in trouble with the law for talking to a white lady, so they took him away then came back and took Bo's mother. The old man told us that he and his wife were fortunate they were old and Bo was too little so them men had no interest in them. Aysen was real strong, and without him they had no way of keeping up with the homestead because it was too much work, so they decided to go east to try to find someone who would take them in.

"You come to village with us," Micco said.

"That's right! You can come with us to the natives' village," I exclaimed. "We'll give you a place to stay!"

Tayki could use some help around the chikee. Bo could help us in the garden, and she'd be real good to him just like she was to me and Nakee. The old lady could help Tayki cook and sew, and the old man could spend time fishing in the creek. They'd enjoy watching Bo grow up in a safe place.

Micco was our friend now, and I was sure glad he asked them folks to come with us. I wondered if village boys would be more accepting, and maybe we could all be friends. The next morning, we were excited to have a place to go, and to tell you the truth, I was feeling a little homesick for the village. Maybe someday I'd leave again, but right then, we were going home. I took a book out of my bag and enjoyed the ride.

THE END